CHILDREN OF SLATE

CHILDREN OF SLATE

Thom Brucie

⚓ENROUTE

ENROUTE
Make the time

ENROUTE

5705 Rhodes Avenue

St. Louis, MO 63109

Contact us at contactus@enroutebooksandmedia.com

Cover by TJ Burdick

Cover credit: main image via pixabay.com at

https://pixabay.com/en/cave-light-person-rocky-silhouette-1835825/

Author photo by Carol Brucie

Library of Congress Control Number: 2018944924

Print ISBN: 978-1-950108-47-3

E-book ISBN: 978-1-7324148-7-7

Printed in the United States of America

1 3 5 7 9 10 8 6 4 2

Most assuredly I say to you,

He who believes in Me,

The works that I do he will do also;

And greater works than these he will do.

John 14:12

WINTER

CHAPTER 1

THE MORNING BELL RANG at 5 am. The senior seminarian opened the dormitory door and turned on the light.

"Benedicamus Domino," he called out. Let us praise the Lord.

The waking students answered, "Deo gratias."

No other words. Night Silence remained in force.

Morgan O'Bryan slid his head under the pillow and pulled the edges tight around his ears. Within his cloth-soft cocoon, Morgan squeezed his eyes against the new day, fighting to hold it back, for recent nocturnal events disrupted his sleep. Nadine Shearwater had invaded his dreams.

Morgan startled to alertness when the five-minute warning bell rang.

He must not be late again for chapel.

He drew his cassock over his head and rolled the legs of his pajamas up so they would not show. He tied the Third Order rope around his waist, slipped on his shoes, and combed his hair with his fingers.

As he ran to the stairs, the large wall clock clicked.

Two minutes.

Rushing, he grabbed the stair-rails with both hands and bounded in one jump down each half flight of steps. When he reached the first floor hallway, the wall clock clicked and showed one minute to reach his seat.

He sprinted to the entrance rotunda and slid on the terrazzo to the chapel entrance. He pulled open one of the eight feet high, three feet wide, mahogany-paneled doors and walked past the public prayer screen just as the bell for morning prayers rang.

Late.

The acoustics of the chapel enhanced the simple beauty of male voices chanting Gregorian hymns, so that, in silence, Morgan's shoes skidding against the floor sounded like steam escaping a locomotive. The rule, when late, required him to kneel on the terrazzo, directly in front of the prayer screen, alone in the long, center aisle. There, he waited for Father Gale to knock twice on the top of his kneeler. Morgan hoped this small indiscretion would not result in a mandatory visit to Father Gale's office.

The ceiling rose as high as the room measured wide, giving the space a feeling of grandeur like Notre Dame, without gold. The religious sat along the walls in oak benches with oak kneelers, built in tiers like a stadium. Austere and unpretentious, the somber piety of the place invited prayer. At the far end of the center aisle, two steps above floor level, the square area of spiritual ceremony comprised of a white marble altar and a crucifix. Above and slightly behind the altar, the life-size crucifix hung from the laminated rafters, suspended, as if floating above the altar's sacred space.

Morgan concentrated on the patience of God, and he asked God to practice now on Father Gale. He did not intend to come late to chapel; he was tired. He had difficulty sleeping, for images of Nadine Shearwater crowded his dreams, keeping him half awake and unrested, until the cold of early morning.

"Please, Lord, I'll do better," he prayed.

Morgan knelt with his back straight, his eyes on the crucifix, managing the muscles of his face in an effort to look penitent. Peripherally, he could see the other students in prayerful focus, they too peripherally watching him. Morgan's friend, Peter DiFlavio, turned his head discreetly and grinned.

Father Gale normally kept the late student kneeling long enough to fidget with the discomfort of guilt.

Father Gale was no ordinary man. Built like a bell, he smoked a pipe and studied psychology. This field of science interested him, especially adolescent psychology. He explored theories of behavior and applied them to these children of God who, confined within the walls of monastic solitude, provided subjects easy to analyze. All students knew that no matter what offense they committed, Father Gale would manage to turn it into a classic example of whatever book he happened to be reading. Father Gale read a great deal, so a student could always look forward to a lengthy lecture if a trip to his office became unavoidable. It is true, however, that all students attempted to elude any such visit.

In addition to his study of psychology, Father Gale perfected a peculiar non-verbal attribute, the ability to raise and lower one eyebrow without moving the other. To express annoyance, his right eyebrow rose, elegantly, like a hairy half moon, and he lifted his upper lip in agreement so that the bare outline of his dull, tobacco-brown teeth emphasized his displeasure. The crease of his nose deepened, and he pulled in his shoulders, which stressed his double chin. Once in this position, he remained motionless. This meant that he wanted to see the student immediately after prayers.

Father Gale raised the right eyebrow at Morgan. Then he tapped the back of the kneeler.

After prayers, the students walked to the refectory for breakfast. They recited a decade of the rosary in Latin as they queued.

Morgan waited out of line, and Father Gale motioned for him to approach.

"Morgan," Father Gale began, "the habit of lateness can indicate the onset of an inhibitive avoidance disorder."

"Yes, Father."

"That could end up in counter cathexis, and then where would we be?"

Morgan said nothing.

"In trouble," Father Gale answered for him. "And," he continued, "the onset of such concern can trigger sleep deprivation, leading to insomnia and even hyper somnolence. Further, insufficient sleep can bring on nightmares which can interfere with daily restfulness and inhibit clear thinking."

"Yes, Father."

"Now, Morgan, let's make sure you are getting enough sleep."

"Yes, Father."

"Good. Now, go eat."

"Yes, Father."

Morgan hurried to catch up with the others. He felt relieved that he did not have to go to Father Gale's office. Who knew what that might entail?

At breakfast, students ate quietly with Night Silence still in force.

As Father Gale finished his coffee, Brother Emile walked up to him and whispered into Father Gale's ear. Father Gale rose, pushed his chair into place against the table and stepped down from the prefect's dais, his large stomach balanced by leaning his shoulders backward. He walked to Morgan's table, and whispered.

"I wish to see you in my office, Morgan."

"Yes, Father. Right now?"

"When you finish eating."

"Yes, Father."

After Father Gale left the refectory, the students at Morgan's table made soft, harassing cat-calls of oohs and aahs. Peter Di Flavio grabbed his neck with his hand, pretending to choke himself. Morgan shook his head, picked up his dishes and placed them in the plastic container near the door.

He walked slowly up the stairs. He worried that Father Gale might ask enough questions that Morgan would reveal his encounters with

Nadine Shearwater. Truthfully, he thought of her often, and he did not, as yet, know what to make of these changes in his emotions. Morgan believed he could survive this lecture as long as Nadine stayed out of the discussion.

He prayed that Father Gale would not keep him beyond the beginning of Latin class. After all, he'd only been late for morning Mass. Certainly Father Gale had nothing more in mind. But Morgan's thoughtful probabilities triggered an anxiety of possibilities, including, perhaps, a discussion of sex which he could only imagine in terms of grotesque references to his id, an area which he guessed existed uncomfortably close to his testicles.

Morgan said a little prayer.

"Please, God, let him be reading about something I've heard of."

He reached the third floor, and walked down the hall to the alcove. The eastern sun shone through the large window and reflected off the polished terrazzo, forming a sun-devised pathway leading to Father Gale's room, located directly to the right of the window.

Father Gale used the front portion of the room as his office, with the traditional sleeping cubical located behind the office wall.

Father Gale left his door open.

As Morgan approached, he heard the priest speaking to someone.

Morgan knocked on the metal frame.

"Come in, Morgan."

Father Gale sat in a large, leather chair, his left hand wrapped around the ivory bowl of a curved pipe. His brown wool cassock draped over the sides of the chair, yet, even helped by this suggestion of flowing material, Father Gale's girth remained unhidden.

Next to the chair, a small end table supported a carousel of pipes, an oblong tobacco pouch, and a postcard.

The only light inside the room came from a tarnished brass lamp which stood between Father Gale's chair and the side table. Although there was a rectangular window in the eastern wall, Father Gale covered it with curtains. He preferred what he termed the more alluring warmth of artificial light since he insisted that truth revealed itself only in that area of light which was protected by shadow. The second person sat in the chair in the shadow against the wall across from Father Gale, and Morgan felt her presence, familiar but uncomfortable, like a shirt too tight or the smell of sulfur. He dared not look, for Father Gale could interpret eye-movement as evidence, either of guilt or innocence, depending upon what he was looking for, so Morgan continued to stare at the priest.

Father Gale enjoyed a relaxed inhale from the pipe. His upper lip rose above the stem to expose a small section of teeth. He exhaled, and with the pipe still in his left hand, he removed it from his mouth and gestured with it toward the postcard.

"Do you know what this is, Morgan?"

Morgan shook his head. Then, thinking he might test Father Gale's mood, he said, "God only knows, Father."

His eyes adjusted to the lack of sunlight, and, with a furtive glance into the shadow, Morgan recognized the other person in the room.

His mother.

She sat quietly, but at his mild impertinence she narrowed her eyes in displeasure.

"Mother," he said.

"Yes, Morgan," Father Gale answered. "Your mother drove all this way because of a somewhat puzzling situation."

Father Gale pointed to the table again and used his pipe-end to emphasize the postcard, which displayed a picture of a hillside with a forest of scotch pine covered with drifts of white snow.

"Do you know what this is?" he repeated.

As Prefect to pre-novitiates, Father Gale exemplified the sinew of moral codes, centuries old, and as a courtesy to ambition, he promulgated its hierarchy, its laws, its insistence on obedience; and

Morgan, knowing this, did not speak.

Father Gale continued. "It's a postcard from a girl named Nadine."

He pulled his lips around the pipe end and inhaled. He removed the pipe, exhaled slowly, making no noise. A delicate stream of thin smoke rose through the dim light.

"You should know the impracticality of inter-sexual relationships. Men who are not to be involved with women must accept certain extra-human disciplines, not the least of which is that if you stay away from the temptation, the temptation will stay away from you. That is to say, my son, that if you keep yourself clear of girls, you will not fall victim to wanting one."

Pausing more for effect than need, Father Gale relit his pipe. His glasses slid to the tip of his nose and came to rest at the base of the ball of flesh God had planted on this blessed prelate's face, having, perhaps, in His wisdom, foreseen that Father Gale's eyes would go bad and he would need a place for spectacles to rest.

"You see, Morgan, as Freud would say, the libido and the id are uncontrollable, and we must learn to act in ways which bring them under control."

Morgan tried to look at him as if he had made sense.

"Yes, Father," he said.

He clasped his fingers together in front of him, since his mother did not approve of him putting them in his pockets. He lowered his head, and he tried to include both his mother and Father Gale in his posture by keeping his head bowed and by moving it back and forth, looking from one to the other.

Father Gale smiled. He turned his attention to Mrs. O'Bryan.

"Having said that, I must reiterate, Mrs. O'Bryan, that it is within norms that a seventeen year old teenage boy might receive a postcard from a girl."

"She sent it because she thought he was already home for Christmas vacation. She thought I wouldn't find out. Do you think I would come here for just any foolishness?"

She wore no hat. Her red hair, the color of summer lady bugs, flowed in thick waves below her shoulders and across her back. The clear taut skin on her face suggested an easy life, but harsh wrinkles around the eyes betrayed her. Nevertheless, she had an attractive face, pleasant and modest, a small nose, dignified eyebrows, a slightly pouty lower lip, and an inviting smile with strong, white teeth. Above all, her eyes commanded attention, alert, blue as a mid-winter's twilight sky, and surrounded by whites of unusual clarity with only a hint of soft pink veins inside, near the nose. She presented a complex mixture of rough beauty, suggestive sensuality, and regal intensity.

Father Gale looked away from her, up toward the ceiling, at the spot where the ceiling and the wall met. He had read in a book on the power of non-verbal suggestion that the display of looking up at that spot and waiting a moment to speak was interpreted by others as a gesture of intelligence. He boldly moved his arm across the front of his body, palm up, to remove the pipe from his mouth. Although he did not intend to appear prideful, the pleasure of performing for this woman showed in his eyes.

Given the mother's firm position regarding the postcard, Father Gale turned to face Morgan.

"Morgan, at this stage in a boy's life there are oedipal issues which can be confusing."

"Morgan doesn't hate his mother!" Mrs. O'Bryan insisted.

"Mother? Well, yes, of course he doesn't," Father Gale assured her. "Let's try a different tack."

He looked thoughtfully again at the ceiling, then continued. "How did you meet this girl?"

"It doesn't matter," Mrs. O'Bryan said.

"Yes. Well, how often do you meet with her?"

"He's not going to meet with her anymore," Mrs. O'Bryan answered.

"Yes, very well. Where do you meet with her?"

"He obviously meets her somewhere near the property," Mrs. O'Bryan said.

"Ah," Father Gale said.

"Don't beat around the bush, Father," she said. "Just tell him that he is not to see her anymore."

"Well," Father Gale conceded, "your mother is right, you know."

Father Gale puffed at his pipe, and hazy shadows from the smoke floated across his face. He lifted a piece of lint from his cassock and dropped it to the floor like a penny into a wishing well.

Finally, he said, "Let's talk about your dreams."

Until that moment, Morgan had felt reasonably safe, believing he might get away with a lecture that required mostly the nodding of his head.

Mercifully, his mother interjected.

"He doesn't want to talk about his dreams. Nothing important ever comes from dreaming."

Exasperated, Father Gale confronted Morgan.

"Morgan," he said, "you're not being very helpful in this inquiry."

"No, you're not," Mrs. O'Bryan added.

Encouraged by Mrs. O'Bryan's endorsement, Father Gale suggested the possibility that Morgan's silence hinted at a mixed receptive-expressive language disorder, but Mrs. O'Bryan assured him it did not.

Father Gale experienced a nearly desperate desire to prove to her the advantages, psychologically speaking, of identifying a symptom. He preferred to give the boy something to think about, something with a name.

"I have it," he said triumphantly. "Separation anxiety."

She shook her head.

"Acute stress disorder?"

She ignored him.

He panicked then, and shouted, "Neglect!"

She made him shudder with a glare that suggested that he might well abandon that word and abolish its use in her presence.

"No. No," he said, "strike that. Oh, dear Lord, I don't know. I just don't know."

He placed his pipe in the tray and shook his head from side to side.

"Father," she said, "with all respect to you, I don't care much for psychology. I don't trust it. It's too sentimental and permissive. Morgan is going to be a priest, and he must stay away from any influence that will interfere with that, especially girls. Do you make it a habit to go on dates with women? Of course not. If you stay away from women, why wouldn't you encourage the same from Morgan?"

Father Gale did not argue. He yielded to her certainty, to her motherly instincts, primitive and perilous.

"Father, would you leave us? I want to speak to Morgan alone."

The priest looked aggrieved at her impertinence, but he nodded in deference to her desire. Obediently, he got out of the chair to leave his own room.

"Close the door behind you, won't you?"

He did.

In the quiet which followed, Morgan relaxed a bit, but without warning his mother began to cry.

"Mother."

He moved closer to her and leaned to touch her, but she raised one hand to stop him, hiding her face with the other.

She sniffled through her nose.

"Morgan, why are you doing this to me?"

"Doing what, mother? What am I doing to you?"

"Hurting me so."

He missed her. He wanted to comfort her, and he wanted comfort from her. Yet, he remained uncertain as to what she wanted from him. Helpless, he lowered his shoulders.

"Morgan, you are special. God has chosen you for the priesthood, and I've sacrificed all my life for you. Is this the way you repay me?"

"No, mother."

"You want to do what's right, don't you?"

"Yes."

"I want you to do what's right, too. This girl doesn't want that. She knows you are off limits, and she just wants something she can't have. She wants to steal your vocation. Remember, many are called, but few are chosen. Do you understand?"

"Yes, mother."

"Will you do what is right and stop hurting me?"

"Yes, mother."

"That's good, Morgan. You must confess."

"Yes, mother."

"Then you will be clean again."

"Yes," he said.

Morgan moved closer to her. He put his arms around her and leaned his head against her shoulder. She touched the back of his head with one hand.

"You're a good son, Morgan. Now go and confess."

He stood away from her and smiled. She motioned to the door, and Morgan opened it.

Father Gale stood at the window.

"My mother thinks I should confess, Father."

"That's a good idea," Father Gale agreed. "You may take some time off from classes. Go find Father Christopher. He's probably in his workshop."

"Yes, Father."

CHAPTER 2

FATHER CHRISTOPHER came from a wealthy Massachusetts family, classically educated, and a trained violinist. After college, God called him to the priesthood. His ordination coincided with the outbreak of World War I. Immediately, he volunteered for Chaplain duty with the American Expeditionary Forces. His unit sailed out of Norfolk on a hot day in August with sea gulls screeching and Father Christopher's family standing by their car to watch. His mother cried.

In only a short time, he discovered that words were powerless tools against the structure of organized brutality. In place of talk, he introduced music.

Along one muddy, bloody trench to the next he stole, on nights of cataclysmic bombardments, through days of exhausting face to face shootings, miraculously close to the haunting green clouds of mustard gas, carrying only his violin. There, from one soldier to the next, from one weary stage to the next, he played, soft sonatinas, inventive rhapsodies, flashy bluegrass, hymns to the dying, hymns to the dead.

The war affected him as it did many others. It drove him crazy.

After two years at the front, he found himself shell-shocked and wrapped in bleached white sheets in a hospital bed in Milano, Italy, attended to by a stout nurse named Sophia. She fluffed his pillow and helped him change his clothes. She fed him and wiped his mouth. She made him laugh, and he regained his physical strength.

He laughed frequently, at colors, at sunrises, at insects.

Sophia could not re-introduce him to normal conversation however.

Every morning Sophia asked him, "How are you this morning?"

Every morning, he laughed, but he did not speak.

On the morning of January 17th, she opened the window to a blast of frigid air.

"There," she said.

She went to his bed to fluff his pillow.

"How are you this morning?"

"Once the game is over, the king and the pawn go back into the same box."

"Father Christopher, you talked," Nurse Sophia exclaimed.

"The best thing that could happen to a person," he told her, "is not to have been born. Unfortunately, this happens to very few."

After that, Father Christopher's recovery ensued, and he developed a mild reputation because he frightened visitors by staring intently into their eyes, seeking, he insisted, evidence of their souls.

When he returned to America, the priests of the order declined the government's offer to place him in a veteran's home, and, instead, assigned Father Christopher to the friary of Saint Francis to act as confessor to the young seminarians.

Morgan first met Father Christopher in the refectory kitchen.

He had been struggling with Geometry, having earned a B on his first-quarter report. He knew his mother would express disappointment, so he began to sneak out of the dorm room after bed check to study near the safety light under the stair landing on the first floor.

One night, he suffered a greater hunger for food than for knowledge, and he crept into the kitchen where he discovered a supply of Brother Emile's sugar cookies and a bottle of chocolate milk on the bottom shelf near the back of the walk-in refrigerator. The refectory area was off-limits to the students, except during meal times. In fact, if he were caught in the kitchen after lights-out, he could be expelled. But hunger drove him, and a certain childlike trust that he would not get caught.

As he sat at the wooden table, he broke one of the cookies, took one half, and dunked it into the milk. When he bit the chewy mixture, he closed his eyes, savoring the sweetness of sugar and chocolate and the texture of soft dough against his teeth and his tongue. When he opened his eyes, Father Christopher stood across the table from him.

Morgan sat straight up. The dense silence of midnight and the sparse night safety-light filled him with a sense of doom. He could not move.

"That looks good," Father Christopher said. "Mind if I join you?"

He sat across from Morgan. He filled a glass with chocolate milk and grabbed one of the cookies from the plate. He broke it, gave it a dunk, and rushed it, dripping with milk, to his mouth.

"Um," he said. He pointed to Morgan with the bit end. "Eat."

Morgan hesitated, keeping his eyes on the priest.

Father Christopher reassured him by pushing the plate of cookies toward him, like a serving of bread at Christmas dinner, but Morgan remained in a state of panic, and he neither ate nor drank.

Father Christopher accepted Morgan's recalcitrance. He seemed content to enjoy the quiet and the treat. When he finished the cookie, he drank most of the chocolate milk, but not all. He placed the glass on the table and wiped his mouth with a napkin.

He stood, shoved his chair into place, but he did not make eye contact with Morgan.

"Am I in trouble?" Morgan asked.

"Be sure to clean up before you leave," Father Christopher said. "Don't want to upset Brother Emile."

Two weeks later Father Christopher decided he wanted a helper in his workshop. He asked for Morgan.

Father Christopher never said a word to Morgan about the cookie incident, but afterwards, at varying intervals, he would ask Morgan, "Are you getting enough to eat, son?"

◆◆◆

Morgan walked through the snow to the workshop, a left over, in-ground, stone-walled area used early on when the order quarried slate from the side of the mountain. The quarry ran parallel to the ancient, glacial stream, and the stream water, clear and full of trout, seeped through the crevices of the quarry and kept the shop in the cool dampness of shaded moisture and the smell of raw earth.

The inside of the workshop remained a near-constant seventy-one degrees. Winter, spring, summer, it didn't matter. The early builders, sensitive to the earth's ability to insulate itself and alert to the power of water to find the path of least resistance, dug the workspace deep enough to keep it warm and close enough to the area of surcharge to keep it cool. Over the years, newer maintenance facilities were built, and the dungeon, as it was called, became the sole domain of Father Christopher and his idiosyncratic projects.

Father Christopher stood at the workbench sharpening a chisel on the grinding wheel. The high-pitched noise bounced metallic off the gray walls. Morgan walked to Father Christopher's side, leaned over the bench to show his face, and waved to the priest.

He finished sharpening the chisel and turned off the grinder.

"Michael," he said. "Is it Saturday already?"

"No, Father. It's Morgan, and I need to confess."

"Ah, yes," Father Christopher said. "I thought it was Saturday, and you came to help."

"No, Father. I've come to confess."

"Are you getting enough to eat, Michael?"

"Yes, Father," he said. "And, Father, it's me, Morgan."

"I'm fine, Morgan, thank you. Look here what I'm making."

Father Christopher pointed to the workbench made of maple planks and scarred with chips and bruises from years of use. A large steel vise was bolted to the front of the table, and near it, placed one next to the other, he saw a small finish hammer, three sharp chisels, and a wooden cross about thirty inches high, held together with brass screws.

"I've been thinking about Christ's wounds," Father Christopher said. "Great debate, you know, whether He was nailed through the hands or through the wrists. Those who argue for the hands insist that nails into the wrists would sever the radial pulse, causing Him to die quickly. Those who argue for the wrist insist that nails in the hand would tear through the skin since the bones run straight to the fingers, but a nail in the wrist would hold Him in place if it went in between the radial and the ulna."

"Father," Morgan said, "I must confess because my mother is here, and I'd like to visit with her."

"I haven't decided which is the better argument," Father Christopher said, "so I'm doing some research. See?"

He held up the cross for Morgan's inspection.

"I made this cross out of pine, soft wood, you know, so I can put nails in and pull them out easily. I've ordered plastic bones from a mail order house, and I'm going to nail them in different positions to make my own determination."

Although the room was cool, Morgan began to sweat since he wore his winter coat. He unbuttoned it and wiped his forehead.

"Father Christopher, why is that important to you?"

"Important? Well, yes, it is important to me, and I'll let you know some other time. Now, what's this about confession?"

"Don't you need your stole?"

"Stole? Oh, no. Not necessary because I don't have one with me."

"Well, if it's okay."

Father Christopher sat on the stool in front of the bench. He motioned for Morgan to sit next to him. Morgan pulled the aluminum lawn chair from next to the wall and sat down.

"What's the problem, Morgan?"

"Bless me, Father, for I have sinned."

"That's fine. Tell me what's going on."

"I've seen a girl, Father."

"Ah," Father Christopher said. He closed his eyes and smiled. "I too have had visions."

"No, Father, not a vision. I mean I have met with her, spoken to her."

"Oh."

"And we exchanged notes. In the tree."

"Notes?"

"Sometimes she leaves a note in the branch of the apple tree. And sometimes I leave one. And sometimes we meet at the tree. When I met her, she was sitting in the tree. She touched me on the cheek."

He hesitated and turned his eyes away from the priest.

"I liked it."

Neither spoke for a moment.

"Is that all?" Father Christopher asked.

"Yes, Father."

"Why do you think your behavior is sinful?"

"Because I'm going to become a priest, with a vow of chastity, and a priest is celibate, and I was tempted."

"What do you mean, tempted?"

"Sometimes I have wondered whether I should become a priest. I'm ashamed. I know I should not give in to such temptations."

"Christ Himself was tempted, but He didn't punish Himself. He reprimanded Satan for the temptation. Perhaps you should do the same."

"But, Father, I'm not Christ."

"No, but we try to live Christ-like lives. That means we follow His example, doesn't it?"

"Yes."

"Okay then. Ego te absolvo. Your sins and your temptations are forgiven. Now go visit your mother."

"That's all?"

"Sure. You want more?"

"What about my penance, Father?"

"Penance. Let's see. Have you taken care of the apple tree? Pruned it? Fertilized it? Granted it a special place in your life?"

"No, Father. I have not."

"Okay, then. Your penance is to prune the apple tree."

"Prune the tree?"

"We'll discuss it later. Run along. I have work to do."

Morgan hesitated.

"Father, was that a real confession?"

"You have a penance, don't you?"

"Yes."

"Then it's a real confession. Now go."

"Okay, Father. Thank you."

Morgan rushed from the shop, through the snow, and into the school building. He charged up the stairs, down the corridor, through the rotunda, and knocked on Father Gale's door.

"Come in."

"It's me, Father Gale. May I visit my mother now?"

Morgan's smile betrayed his excitement, and he looked around the room.

"Your mother left, Morgan. She said there were others at home, and you must attend to your studies. She said she will see you soon, when you go home for Christmas."

"Oh," he said.

He looked at the floor, saw there nothing but a puzzling array of carpet patterns, meaningless and random.

"She's quite a woman, your mother," Father Gale said.

Morgan ignored him and walked out of the room.

CHAPTER 3

IN THE ALCOVE, Morgan leaned against the wall and pushed his forehead against it as if he might see through it to her, as if he might look in upon her and she would smile at him. But the wall offered no such vision, its cool plaster and slick gray paint merely a barrier.

"Mother," he whispered.

He did not go to class. He could not reconcile his need for comfort with the molasses dullness of conjugated Latin verbs.

The building seemed empty, like that part of him that missed his family, that part of him that missed the daily comfort of home and brothers and the security of his parents' voices; that emptiness that he could not talk about, to them, or to anyone.

He went to his room, removed his jacket, and looked out the window. The snow had come early in November, and continued, piling upon itself, innate and thick, lugubriously white and unseamed. He felt the cold outside and the bitterness of it. His cheerless exhales frosted the frigid glass, and the hollowness of his breaths made him more alone. The silence of the room became empty architecture which acted to isolate him instead of to insulate him.

Normally, he controlled the melancholy, fought it, forced his teeth together and made his jaw hard to crush it. He cradled the melancholy deep in the empty center of his stomach, locked away, and sometimes he could ignore it by activities like baseball and conversation.

But solitude germinates voids that must be filled by memory, that uncivilized function of the brain, imprudently ruthless in its excessive, romantic need for emotion. He let his memory go to Nadine, and he decided to go out, into the snow, across the hill, to the cluster of apple trees where he first met her. He knew this rebellion would give Father Gale an opportunity to examine him. Skipping classes demonstrated highly irregular behavior, and he could only guess what Freud might have to say about it.

He grabbed his coat and pushed his arms through the sleeves. The ceremony of dress consoled him. He buttoned the coat, pulled it against himself, surrounded his arms and chest with the cloth of it. He tightened the collar around his neck and pushed the rough wool against his ears. Then he pulled on a hat, knotted a scarf around his neck, and left the room, carrying his gloves and a growing uncertainty about God's plan for him.

As he opened the door to the outside, a sharp wind reddened his face. He felt the bitter spark of life, inhaling freezing air, crystallizing the emptiness in his stomach like ice forming over shallow water.

The snow was intensely white, and the sun created oblong patterns of bluish reflections that looked as if lights shone from within the hollows. Even in sadness, he marveled at the artistic hand of God, and he imagined that God found pleasure in beauty and that He laughed with delight at His creations. The vitality of his union with God changed when he met Nadine and she smiled at him, and she laughed at his awkwardness, and she touched his cheek with her fingertips. He shuddered when he thought of her hand on his skin; yet the thought freed his melancholia and made him smile.

He walked past the square, brick gymnasium and continued along the knoll, pushing his boots through the snow, watching the brittle skeletons of the trees shiver in the moaning wind. The trees of the orchard grew along the backside of the knoll. Among them, within their shade, atop their fallen leaves, against their meaty trunks, he felt safe. On the backside of the knoll, the school buildings fell out of sight, and the playing fields, also out of sight, the tennis courts, handball courts, bright lights, candle lights, candle ends, dead ends, empty rooms – all out of sight. For this reason, because of the safety and privacy of his grotto, Nadine's casual appearance and simple approach was now a part of it for him. Besides the trees and the safety and the solitude must be added Nadine with her smile and her danger.

He fell backward into the soft snow. The crunch of the powdery explosion felt alive in his ears. He sank into a depression, and the snow surrounded him, packed under him and contoured along his side, around his arms, over the top of his legs so that only the tips of his boots protruded like two brown groundhogs searching for spring. The scarf and the snow muffled the wind. The trees dropped excess snow from their branches. The sun made shadows. No bird sang.

He wished that Nadine would walk around the corner, right now, intentionally seeking him, for he could not seek her.

Wishing helped him pass the time; yet it did not occur to him that time was passing. The sun moved, the clouds changed their secretive shapes, but Morgan took no notice. Lured into a meditation, with his brain caressed by airy memory, his pain abated. In mindless relaxation, he lay in the snow under the pressure of cold insulated by clothing, feeling the same as he might feel if he were suspended within a frozen sea. He squeezed his eyelids and saw the miraculous brightness of a shocking, white starfish undulating in his head. The cold air grazed the skin on his face. His hot breath trembled the scarf at his mouth. And Morgan, neither asleep nor awake, remembered the first time he met her.

◆◆◆

In the early years of the order, the apple orchard supplied food for the community with enough excess to sell at a roadside market, thus acting as a profit center. By the 1950s, donations and missionary preaching far exceeded income from farming, and the trees in the apple orchard grew wild, their dark-barked trunks surrounded by twisted, cross-grown branches which resembled the knotty, misshapen fleshiness of fig trees. Wild grapes braided thick, rope-like, python-slow vines through the trees, and on full moon nights they took on the added sadness of moaning cedars after being struck by lightning. The unpruned branches and stringy leaves drew nourishment away from the fruit, and the apples grew small with green leathery skins on the outside and tiny black fruit worms on the inside, but the deer herd ate them and the wind-fall helped thicken their coats for winter.

Not everyone appreciated the orchard as Morgan, but within this combination of nature's insulation and isolation, he rested. He thought of it perhaps as his outdoor chapel, or perhaps he claimed it as a place of solitary familiarity. That is why he reacted in shock at her intrusion.

She sat on the first strong branch, an unusually thick limb for an apple tree, plump as pewter, and strong. The leaves had begun to change color, crispy and curled, shuddering in the breeze like quaking aspen. She sat composed, in blue jeans and a white sweat shirt. Her long black hair draped down and across one shoulder, while the sunlight triggered silver and indigo highlights. She had a slightly round face with smooth skin. Her small nose rose at its end and compressed the muscles of her top lip. This exposed her teeth and made her look happy even if she wasn't smiling. She appeared fearless, as if her act of trespass must be overlooked for no reason other than she expected it.

When he walked over the ridge and into the grove, she tilted her head, not as gesture so much, but more as a photographer might in order to ascertain foreground and background.

Morgan thought he might be looking at an angel.

"Hello," she said.

Her voice struck Morgan as soft female music, like the unexpected note of a flute escaping from within the trees.

"Hello," he managed, but he moved his eyes away from her to the ground. He fidgeted with his hands because he did not know what to do with them.

She smiled at his shyness. Perhaps she sensed that she might influence him one way or another, toward fear or away from it. She jumped down from the tree and landed with supple soundlessness.

Morgan felt a surge of tingles along his arms, for she was alien to him and to his space. Yet, she seemed a natural part of the trees and the grass.

As she approached him, she smiled a sign of invitation. A slight breeze lifted and dropped the end strands of her hair. When she reached him, the aphrodisiac smell of over-ripe apples filled his nose.

"Hey," she said. "Who are you?"

Morgan bit his teeth together, and his jaw muscles trembled from the pressure for he did not know what to say.

She tilted her head to the right, a gesture intended to encourage him to speak.

"My name is Morgan O'Bryan," he said, and he took a step back.

"My name is Nadine Shearwater." She stuck out her hand to shake.

Morgan did not reach for her hand, but he waved and nodded.

"I live over there," she continued, pointing beyond the orchard. "You're from the school, I guess."

She spoke without raising her voice, with little undulation to the rhythm.

"Yes," he said.

She looked away, perhaps to ease Morgan's discomfort, and he, too, looked around, at the sky above the tree tops, at the ground.

Finally, they both spoke at once.

"What are you doing here?" they asked, combining voices.

He apologized. "Sorry, I didn't mean . . ."

"That's okay," she said. "I like to come here. I like the trees and the view. And I can get away from things."

"But it's private property."

"So? I'm not hurting anything."

"But you're not supposed to be here."

"Why?"

"This is a seminary."

"I like being naughty."

"Well, you shouldn't be here. Girls aren't allowed. I could get in trouble."

"Why would you get in trouble for something I do?"

It seemed like a reasonable question, and he could conjure no sensible answer.

"I don't know. I just will."

She curled her hair away from her ear. "If you don't come around no one will see me, and you won't get into trouble."

"But I come here all the time. You should stop coming."

"But I come here all the time, too," she persisted. "Tell you what, if you don't tell, I won't tell."

He shook his head. "You're funny."

"Deal then?"

"Yeah," he said. "I guess."

They shook hands.

Without intent, as a natural consequence of curiosity and close proximity, they looked into one another's eyes. Softly. Almost tenderly.

"Thanks," she said. "You're sweet."

She lifted her hand and touched his cheek.

She turned and walked away toward her home.

"Maybe I'll see you again," she said.

He watched her disappear past the treeline and through the invisible barrier of the property line.

"Okay," he said, but he said it only in his head because the touch changed him.

He wondered if she knew that her touch startled him or that it cracked the crusty restriction around his heart that forbade touch? Could she have guessed that his mother had prophesied that he would find the surest sinful path to hell at the hand of a woman?

Morgan knew the fervor with which his mother protected him, and he understood her fear because Nadine's touch did not feel like sin.

He continued to lie in the snow. Yet, a cocoon of unfulfilled wishes lasts only as long as the heart can tolerate uninterrupted pleasure, and although he enjoyed the destitute bliss of remembrance, the cold crept upon him and began to turn his blood to jelly. The frozen ground and the relentless chill within the snow penetrated the layers of clothing like deadening fingers. His mind remained half in a state of dreamy gloom, unaware of a drop in body temperature, and he might have remained there, suspended in a state of bewildered hypothermia had he not felt a carnal and inappropriate sensation along his thighs. The feeling, erotic and physical, snapped his lethargy, and he opened his eyes to the blurry, distorted image of Peter Di Flavio.

"What are you doing?" Morgan asked.

"What are you doing?" Peter countered. "We missed you in classes this morning. It's lunch time already."

Morgan shivered.

"Man, you're freezing," Peter said. "Let's get to the infirmary before you get sick."

Peter offered his hand.

Morgan grabbed it. When he stood, he went dizzy, and his muscles quivered from the cold.

Peter pulled Morgan's arm over his shoulder to help him walk.

"You're heavy," Peter said.

Morgan trudged silently.

"What's going on, Morgan? You've never tried to kill yourself before."

"My mother was here."

"I don't see her footprints. You were dreaming."

"No. She was here. In Gale's room. Nadine sent a post card to my house."

"Oh. This is about Nadine. Watch your step."

"She thinks she's trying to steal my vocation."

"Too many pronouns in that sentence. You better rest."

Morgan shook his head.

Peter's nickname was Adonis, after the Greek god of beauty. Adonis was a physically beautiful youth, but he lived half of his afterlife in the light above ground and half of his afterlife below, in the nether world, thus signifying good and evil. It was generally conceded that Peter was the most handsome youth at the school, but he did have an ironic wit that bordered on the nether side.

They walked to the basement, past the refectory, to the infirmary.

Brother Emile looked up from his desk.

"What happened?" he asked.

"Nothing serious," Peter said. "He fell asleep in the snow. Probably there a couple of hours. I think he's cold."

"Thanks," Morgan said, returning the sarcasm.

"Sit here," Brother Emile said.

He put a thermometer in Morgan's mouth.

"Let's see what we've got."

Brother Emile checked Morgan's pulse.

"Your pulse is low."

Morgan continued to shiver.

"Temperature is 96.8. Too low. Peter, will you get his things? Pajamas, slippers, tooth brush?"

"Sure, Brother. I'll bring them right down."

"Morgan, let's get you out of these clothes and into bed."

Brother Emile helped Morgan into the first of three infirmary rooms.

Morgan felt light headed as he took off his coat. Twinkling lights flashed in an oblong pattern in front of his eyes. He reached for the bed to steady himself, but he missed the frame and fell to the floor.

Later, when he awoke, the village doctor stared down at him.

"You're awake," he said. "I think you'll be okay, but you need rest." He turned to Brother Emile. "I've been telling Father Gale for years these kids study too hard. Half the time I come here it's for exhaustion. This time, it's for exhaustion and for not knowing enough to come in out of the cold." He shook his head. "Well, Brother Emile, you know the drill. Keep him warm and dry. Give him warm liquids and thin soup for the next twenty-four hours. Call me if he doesn't improve."

The two men walked out.

Peter sat in the chair.

"I can't stay long. Brother Emile said only a minute."

"Thanks for helping, Pete."

"My pleasure. Not often I get to undress my best friend."

Morgan blushed.

"Hey, somebody had to."

"Well, thanks," Morgan said.

"No problem. Actually, Brother Emile did most of the work. But I did help."

"Yeah."

"I'll see you tomorrow. Try to sleep."

Morgan relaxed. The down pillow fluffed around his ears and held firm against his neck. The fluorescent light fixtures gave the room's beige walls a strong tint of yellow. Morgan pulled the covers up to his chin. What an interesting day, he thought just before he fell asleep.

By morning, the chills subsided, although the tips of his fingers remained numb.

Brother Emile brought a breakfast of hot tea with one packet of sugar but no milk. Morgan sipped the tea, but he felt tired and began to fall asleep after drinking only half the cup.

Suddenly, the lights came on and with them a bright scarlet glare bubbled behind his eyelids. He covered his eyes and simultaneously nudged the food tray with his elbow.

"Good morning, Morgan," Father Gale said. "Brother Emile said you were looking better. The color is back in your face. How do you feel?"

"I feel fine, Father."

Morgan blinked and looked at the priest. He tried keeping eye contact, but he worried that Gale intended to psychoanalyze him. He didn't want that, so he stared at the blanket and tried to look sick.

"Good," he said. "I thought you reacted yesterday more acutely than I might have liked, what with the postcard and your mother's visit. You could be experiencing an anxiety disorder with melancholic features."

"Yes, Father."

"I'd like to talk with you more about it when you're feeling stronger."

"Yes, Father."

"Until then, stay in the infirmary. Brother Emile will keep me posted."

Morgan looked quizzically at the prelate, uncertain of what motives might drive such an offer, and wondering, too, whether a few extra days of rest would impact his grades.

"What about my classes?" he asked.

"You're doing well enough. I'm sure your teachers will bring your assignments. A good rest might be just the thing; some time to pray and think."

"Yes, Father."

"Good, then. I'll check in on you from time to time."

"Thank you, Father."

CHAPTER 4

THE NEXT DAY, the feeling in Morgan's finger tips had not returned, and he remained tired and morose.

Late in the afternoon, Father Christopher stopped to see him.

"How are you feeling, Morgan?"

"Much better."

"Good. You had us worried."

Morgan lowered his eyes.

"You look fine now."

Morgan continued to experience a strange feeling of interior chills, especially in his arms and in the heels and toes of his feet, as if he were cold inside his body instead of outside on his skin. But he thought that might be from inactivity or the chilly cement of the infirmary walls, so he didn't say anything.

Suddenly, Father Christopher grabbed Morgan's hand and shook his arm.

Morgan let it flop in answer to the unusual movement, and when Father Christopher let go, the arm plopped against the mattress.

Immediately, all chills left Morgan. His body temperature returned to normal, and his heart again beat with the rhythm of a healthy seventeen year old.

"What did you do?" he asked.

"Something you must learn."

"My chills are gone."

"Yes."

"And I feel energetic, like I could run a circle around the school."

"Of course."

"How did you do that, Father?"

"I didn't do anything. The Lord did."

"The Lord?"

"Can't explain now. Busy. Work to do."

Father Christopher left.

Morgan rubbed his arms. They felt muscular and warm. He pulled the blankets away and stood.

Not dizzy.

"Wow," he said.

He decided to shower, and the water splashed against his skin, tingling and exuberant.

He washed his hair.

He felt like singing.

He walked out of the shower to discover Father Gale standing at the doorway.

"Mr. O'Bryan," he said.

Morgan wrapped the towel around himself.

"Why aren't you in bed, resting?"

"I took a shower."

"Did Brother Emile suggest it?"

"No."

"You did so on your own?"

"Yes, Father."

"Why, please?"

"I feel good, Father. I'm much better."

"Oh? How do you explain that?"

Morgan lowered his eyes. "I'm not sure."

"I trust we are not dealing with a factitious disorder," Father Gale said.

51

"Father Christopher visited."

Father Gale raised an eyebrow.

"He…"

"He shook your arm, perhaps?"

"Yes, but how did you know?"

"Some mysteries must wait for discovery."

"Father?"

"Morgan, I suggest you remain in the infirmary the rest of today and tonight. If you feel the same enthusiasm of good health in the morning, perhaps you should go to work with Father Christopher. Tomorrow is Saturday, and by performing your work assignment, it will help you get back into your normal routines."

"Yes, Father. But how did you know?"

"I suspect Father Christopher has an assignment in mind for you."

"What do you mean, Father?"

"Time will tell. Dress warm and rest."

"Yes, Father."

Morgan decided to brush his teeth.

What happened to me? And how did Father Gale know?

Maybe Father Christopher would explain things in the morning.

When he was ready for bed, he felt hungry. He walked down the hall to the refectory to ask Brother Emile for an early supper. To his surprise, a plate of meatloaf, mashed potatoes, green beans, two slices of buttered bread, and two glasses of milk awaited him.

"Father Gale thought you might stop by."

"Thank you, Brother."

Morgan carried the tray to the infirmary. He put the food on the hospital tray and sat on the bed to eat.

To his surprise, when he finished eating, and after he drank one glass of milk, he felt tired.

He pushed the food away from the bed, laid his head against the pillow, and he fell asleep outside the blankets. He slept soundly all night.

In the morning, he showered again. He organized his clothing, stripped the bed, and took his belongings to the dorm. By the time he finished, it was time for work crew, and he hurried to the workshop.

Father Christopher stood at the workbench. He had placed, side by side, pruning shears and a branch saw.

"Good Morning, Father. It's Morgan."

"How are you?"

"I'm better, thank you. How did you do that arm shaking thing with me?"

"Yes," he said. "You need some exercise. It's time you complete your penance."

"My penance?"

"You know, the tree."

"Oh. But, Father, what about you shaking my arm?"

"Different lesson today, Morgan. Do you know how to prune a fruit tree?"

"No, Father."

"Here. You'll need these." He handed Morgan the shears and the saw.

"Father Gale knew before I told him. How did he know?"

"First thing, those old trees have too many dead branches. Dead branches have cuts in the bark and hard, dry twigs. Start by removing all of them. Cut at an angle like this."

Father Christopher slanted his right hand and moved it back and forth like a saw blade.

"I see."

"Then get as close as you can to the trunk and look up through the branches. Sucker branches grow straight up, and they won't hold fruit. Cut them off."

"Yes, Father."

"Next, trim the excess branches. Choose them by picturing the sun shining through. Every branch that blocks the sun from the branch below, cut it. Finally, use the clippers to form the tree. Cut the outside and top into an umbrella shape. Got that?"

"Yes, Father."

"In the spring, that tree will have less fruit than the trees around it, but the fruit will be bigger and juicier. Next fall, prune it again. After that, the tree will bear the best fruit in the orchard."

"Okay, Father."

"Be sure to clean up after yourself. Cut all the trimmings into small pieces and scatter them at the base of the tree. That will keep the roots warm during the winter, and when they rot, they make fertilizer."

"I will, Father."

"And bring the step ladder."

"Yes, Father."

◆◆◆

Morgan carried the tree saw, the pruning shears, and the step ladder to the apple orchard. When he arrived at their tree, he leaned against the trunk and looked up to the sky. A few crinkled leaves clung to the branches, and the growth patterns of the limbs, like the arthritic legs of an old spider, criss-crossed so that several of them seemed to grow into one another. Some branches looked dead, cracked and dull, but without spring buds he could not be certain which were dead and which fallow. The riddle of growth looked like different sized ropes tangled into knots, black and craggy in the deciduous grip of winter.

He decided to begin with crooked or damaged wood, branches that were split or broken in some way. He chose a large branch near the seat of the tree. The saw made a smooth sound, and sawdust sprinkled atop the snow like brown sugar. The lifeless wood cut easily. Morgan cut a second, smaller branch. He climbed onto the branch Nadine liked to sit on. From there, he severed a broken branch above his head and two additional, smaller ones, but these caught in the tree. He climbed higher to grab the branches and dropped them to the ground.

He began to sweat, and he loosened his scarf. With the obvious dead branches removed, he could see areas of cross growth and some sucker branches that rose straight as small flag poles. He wondered why uncontrolled growth minimized productive growth. Father Christopher told him that farmers keep nature in a state of perpetual adolescence. If they didn't prune, disc, cut, mow, and re-seed, every farm would become a forest, eventually.

As he studied the array of branches, he grew more comfortable with his task.

He lifted the pruning shears, sharp as a hunting knife. He cut a sucker, then another, and another.

He tried to imagine the sun heating and nourishing each major branch, each limb, each tiny twig so that spring buds would sprout and blossom to ripe fruit. If he looked from different angles, he could guess where one branch might impede another, and he cut. He guessed that the end of branches, with two or sometimes three sprouted twigs would weigh too heavily for healthy growth, and he cut the lesser ones, leaving what he perceived were the strongest.

Slowly, but with an increasing sense of accomplishment, he pruned.

He circled the trunk one last time, inspecting, judging. He decided to cut one final limb. As he stood on his toes and lifted the shears, Nadine appeared, and her appearance startled him.

"Morgan, what are you doing?"

She wore a tight red coat with a fox fur collar, and the delicate hairs of the collar nestled against her chin and mingled within her hair. Her face seemed a little red, maybe from the cold.

Nadine's proximity filled him with uncertainty because of the vow to his mother, and his emotions felt like tangled branches, twisted and grown wild.

He turned his head upward and snapped a near branch with the trimmers. He forced the wooden handles with some urgency, yanking the sharp claws from between the living tree and the severed branch.

"Morgan, are you going to talk to me?"

"I'm busy, Nadine. I can't talk right now."

"What's the matter, Morgan?"

Morgan cut another branch, pruning now to appear busy, rather than to encourage rejuvenation.

"Okay," Nadine said. "See you later."

He watched her walk under the branches, around the trees, making tracks in the snow, ignoring him. He lowered the shears and used the back of his glove to wipe sweat from his forehead.

"That's enough," he said aloud.

He took the shears and began to cut the thin branches into small pieces to lay at the base of the tree. For a time, the sun shone, and his shadow reminded him of a silent puppet, moving along his tracks, gliding over and through the mounds of fallen branches and twigs that lay like puzzle pieces in the snow.

A penance is a penance, he thought, and he knew the attitude of penance brought forgiveness as much as the penance itself. He wasn't sure this principle represented Christ's teaching, but that's why he was in school, to learn. Father Christopher often managed to mix him up, for example telling him he didn't really sin when he talked to Nadine, but what about his mother? What about her?

Maybe Father Christopher was crazy after all.

He finished piling the trimmings around the tree, and he stacked the larger branches which he could not cut with the shears. He would carry them to the fire pit. He gathered the pruning shears and the saw, and Nadine walked out from behind a nearby tree.

"Okay, Morgan, what's going on?"

"Nadine, I can't talk to you."

"Why not?"

"I just can't," he said.

Nadine tilted her head at him and gave him a look which combined reproach with expectation, her face, smooth and delicate, strong and indignant.

However, their eyes lingered, and Morgan felt his stomach go skittish.

"Okay," she said, and she began to walk away again.

"Wait, Nadine."

She stopped and faced him.

"My mother brought the card you sent."

"Did you like it?"

"I didn't get to read it."

"Why not?"

"Nadine, I'm trying to tell you something."

"What?"

"My mother thinks you are trying to hurt me, and Father Gale said it's not a good idea to let a girl tempt me."

Nadine took a step closer to him, close enough for their exhaled breaths to mingle.

"Tempt you?" Her eyes fluttered. "Why, Morgan, do I tempt you?"

"Stop that," he said, but he said it with a grin. She made him happy; he couldn't help it.

"What are you doing to our tree? Why are you cutting it all up? Are you going to destroy it because it's a temptation too?"

"No. I'm pruning it."

"What for?"

"I have to."

"You have to?"

"I can't talk about it. It's private. From confession."

"I don't understand."

"I went to confession. This is my penance. Now I've told you. I don't think I'm supposed to tell anyone my penance. I've got to go."

He started to leave.

"Wait," Nadine said, and she touched his shoulder to hold him. "What did your mother say?"

"What?"

"I want to know. How am I hurting you?"

"She said you were trying to steal my vocation."

Nadine inched closer to Morgan, heating the space around him.

"No," she insisted, "I'm not trying to steal your vocation. I'm stealing this!"

She grabbed the trimming shears and walked into the shadows toward her home.

"I didn't say it," Morgan said. "She did," like a whisper, thinking that this conversation hadn't gone exactly as he might have wished. Besides, what will Father Christopher say about the missing shears?

The next day, before he left for Christmas break, he put a note in the tree.

Dear Nadine,

I'm sorry. I didn't mean to hurt you. Have a nice life.

Morgan

CHAPTER 5

MORGAN RODE the bus home along a two-lane roadway bounded by rolling hills and the fallow, leafless red maple and white oak trees and the evergreen pinnacles of Douglas fir and Scotch pine. This trip reminded him of the first drive to St. Francis. He was fourteen when he left home, with his father, riding in a car toward his uncertain future. His mother did not accompany them, nor his brothers.

Since that day, the homesickness made him hurt in the way of longing for something once loved, now gone. He feared, at times, the feeling of loneliness might kill him. It did not kill him; neither, however, did it leave him. Eventually, he accepted it, as he accepted that his hands grew, or his hair.

That first trip, he was young and naive. He did not know what his decision to enter the seminary would bring. He wanted his father or his mother to tell him. Naturally, neither had the experience or the words to explain the consequences of such a choice.

The drive lasted three hours. The long miles of silence and endless forest solitude brought on a desire to have his father stop the car and return home.

He wanted to cry, "Stop."

He wanted to change his mind, change his decision. He wanted to go home, and the ensuing idealization of home grew profound.

Each Christmas break, he rode the bus home, each journey a perilous two week confrontation between his past and his unknown future. And this trip, full of the coming and going of Nadine Shearwater, this third year of his independence and his training, this year he added doubt to homesickness, and he could not reconcile his longing to serve God and his longing for human love.

He folded a sweat shirt to use as a pillow, and he leaned his head against the window. The glass felt cold in spite of the insulation of his shirt. He sensed the passing landscape of hillsides, speeding into and out of his vision, passing like days, hurried and inscrutable.

He slept intermittently, relaxing with the monotonous rhythm of spinning wheels against the frozen, winter road.

At last he arrived in Galeton, and the sight of the sooty, brick buildings of downtown comforted him. He was home. Maybe here he could clarify his options.

His mother stood in a line of people waiting for arriving travelers. He waved to her. She smiled, stood a little straighter, and touched the top of her purse with her right hand.

The bus terminal resonated with memories of Morgan's going away and of his returns; not home, but a representation of it, a place he never visited for any reason except as a stop-off point, and in spite of the impersonal architecture of rectangles, the hard, wooden benches, and the disorganized lines of people, he liked the place. It provided a momentary refuge where he could be ordinary, and his mother did not need to display him, and briefly, among strangers, they united as mother and son.

He put both arms around her, reaching against the bulk of her winter coat to pull himself to her, and she held him.

When they separated, she noticed his socks showed below his pant legs. She looked intently at his face and at the top of his head.

"Morgan," she said, "you've grown a foot since summer. It's odd I didn't notice in Father Gale's office."

He looked down, but he had no answer for her observation. He had not grown a foot, of course, but he had sprouted several inches.

"Pick up your bag," she said. "Let's go home."

She drove her sister's car, a two-tone, cashmere blue and ivory, 1953, hard top, Chevy Bel-Air. Her sister, Morgan's Aunt Lillian, remained the only unmarried adult member of the family. She had been a nun for two years, after high school, and it made her parents proud. Eventually, however, she decided against vows, and this decision so shocked her parents that they refused to let her live in their home, since they harnessed such a choice to the influence of the devil. Lillian, in an effort to support their superstitions, got a job as a secretary, bleached her hair blond, and wore red lipstick. She cultivated some local renown as a woman with a special fondness for black-haired Irishmen and for ostentatious cars. The Bel-Air was her latest.

They rode in silence. Each street, each corner house, he knew. Past the general store, past the small parish school building, each brought a stronger feeling of the security of childhood.

The snow stopped falling when they arrived at their home, and Mrs. O'Bryan asked Morgan to shovel the front sidewalk. Wrapped in his wool coat, cotton scarf, red hat with flaps that covered his ears, gloves, and rubber boots, he felt useful and needed, like a son. He loved being home, but his position as the only seminarian in a village of immigrant Catholics made him a celebrity, like a saint, and living up to the expectations of sainthood often left him frustrated. He wanted to talk about this with his parents, but the time never seemed right.

He pushed the shovel and threw the snow to the side. He exhaled smoky breaths from his nose. The shovel felt comfortable, the snow compact.

In front of him, past the sidewalk, past the road, beyond the rough, cement retaining wall, he watched the swirling, random floes of gray ice shifting along the river. In the summers, as children, they swam and ran along the banks. In the deep freezes of winter, they skated against the ice which covered the shallow water of the inlets, and the older children kept the warming fire burning in the 55-gallon barrel they used as a stove.

But those were the memories of childhood, no longer a part of his days.

He finished shoveling the short walkway, and he looked up from his work at their house. One of nearly two dozen in a row along the west bank of the river, squat and square, built on twelve inch skids, old timbers from the mines. "If they could hold up the earth, they can hold up a house," the elders said, said it repeatedly, until even they believed it.

Their first house stood further up the hill, and lay abandoned, like the rest. The old houses, lean-tos framed against the smooth hillside after the road had been cut, stood in the umber nakedness of winter like dry stalks split by frost. The families moved to the new homes before Morgan turned five, and the next year he started school, so he had no real memories of the old house, and his mother convinced him that the new one, next to the river, square and solid, two stories tall, with one bedroom for his parents and another for the children on the second level, constituted an improvement and represented a move toward wealth. In this house they did not share space with another family. In this house they became Americans; and for Morgan, this house, sided with asbestos sheets made to look like brown bricks with black mortar joints, felt different than the rest. This house was his home.

As he cleaned up the last few spots, Carol O'Malley, returning from school, called to him. He waved. Their friendship, lifelong, changed when he went away. She treated him with a reserve children normally save for adults. He was different now, a man of the cloth. He wished for his childhood when they ran and played with no embarrassment.

"School must be out. John and Gabriel will be home soon."

He shook the last of the snow from the shovel and looked over his effort.

"Okay," he said.

He walked to the back of the house into the porch area behind the kitchen. He hung his coat and hat and removed his boots. The kitchen began to smell like dinner. Water boiled, and Mrs. O'Bryan washed vegetables in the sink.

Morgan proceeded past the bookcase that divided the living room from the kitchen, separating the formal from the casual. The kitchen side of the bookcase was boarded over with horizontal strips of one-by-six shiplap pine, and the open side of the case faced the living room.

The O'Bryans reserved the first book shelf for three icons: a statue of the blessed Virgin, her foot crushing the head of the serpent; a votive candle, which they lit on the first Friday of every month; and a miniature plaster cast of a smiling leprechaun in a blue coat with tails and a top hat. On the second shelf, they kept a cigar box which stored their letters; a small, oddly rectangular stone, which reminded Mr. O'Bryan of the blarney stone; and three books, an illustrated copy of *The Book of Irish Legends: All of Which are True,* a leather-bound copy of *Lives of the Saints*, which Mr. O'Bryan prized, and a family Bible which belonged to Mrs. O'Bryan's grandmother, and passed to her from her own mother on her wedding day. This relic contained not only the sacred scripture, but the baptismal and death dates of nearly one hundred members of her clan, the most recent listings, of course, being the deaths of her parents and the births of her own three sons. The bottom shelf they left empty as a storage area where the boys could leave their books when they came home from school.

Morgan sat in the chair across from the bookcase and admired the creeping Charlie that Mrs. O'Bryan kept on the side table next to the chair. Its long, leafy stems hung down both sides of the table, adding greenery to the living room. Next to the plant, Mrs. O'Bryan displayed an umber sepia Daguerreotype of her mother and father posed in front of their small, stone church in Kenmare, Ireland. The picture was set in an oval cast-metal frame, and every February 1st, on Saint Brigid's Day, she placed a traditional straw-cross against the frame. During the spring of each year, she cut branches of purple lilacs and put them in a water glass next to the picture. Lilacs were one of the few things in America that reminded her of Ireland, lilacs and lilies of the valley. They made her think of church steeples and mossy waterfalls and lush streams which flowed into the dark, blue bay.

John and Gabriel arrived home together. The brothers hugged each other and made noises, mostly simple words. *How are you? Good to see you. Morgan! John! Gabriel!* But spoken by all three at once so that the words blended into one another, and Mrs. O'Bryan shouted above the cacophony, "Boys, go to your room and talk. I can't hardly hear myself think."

The boys laughed.

John and Gabriel left their books on the bottom shelf, and they all walked upstairs to their bedroom. Gabriel, the youngest, closed the door and smiled at Morgan.

"I'm so glad you're home, Morgan," he said.

"Can it," John said, but Morgan rubbed Gabriel's head and the two of them sat on Morgan's bed.

White-washed clapboard covered the walls of the room, and the ceiling was finished with two-foot strips of gypsum lath, unpainted. They used no plaster, and the seams showed.

John lay on the bunk bed that he and Gabriel shared before Morgan left for the seminary. Gabriel slept on top, but when Morgan was gone, John claimed Morgan's small bed.

The boys looked like brothers. They all shared their father's nose, thin and prominent. Morgan and Gabriel had blue eyes, and John had a golden hazel color that changed shades depending on his mood. They all inherited their mother's curved eyebrows and thick hair.

Gabriel attended St. Patrick's Elementary School. He was ten and in fifth grade. He idolized Morgan, and of the three boys, only he had freckles.

"Are you working hard in school, Gabe?" Morgan asked.

"Sure," he said. "Sister Caritas says I might be first in class like you were."

As he spoke, Gabe pushed the first two fingers of his right hand with the palm of his left. He could bend the fingers far enough back to touch his wrist.

"Stop that," Morgan said.

Gabriel grinned, and pushed a little harder. It was a nervous twitch, but he was double-jointed, and he knew it looked painful and disgusting.

"Yeah, that's good, Gabe," John said. "You try to be just like Morgan. At least one of us will."

"What's the matter, John? Still trying to outdo me in school?"

John sat up and dropped his legs over the edge of the bed. Only ten months younger than Morgan, he looked older. His hair was light brown, compared to Morgan's, and he was the same height as Morgan, but he was built like their grandfather, square jawed and sinewy. His face was smooth and his eyes didn't blink when he stared.

The young muscles in his arms rippled when he gestured, the tendons that strengthened his neck formed a V at his throat.

John was the handsome one, for sure, and Morgan knew it. Even Gabe, at his young age, knew it.

"You know I love you, brother," John said, "but I hate following you. These last couple of years everybody's on my case to be like Morgan. Get good grades like Morgan. Play soccer like Morgan."

"I never thought about things like that. I don't mean to make your life difficult." He looked away from John's stare to the plastic crucifix on the opposite wall.

"It ain't you, Morgan. It's Ma. She's always on my case. Nags me all the time. I can't please her for shit."

"Well, just tell her you're not me."

"Yeah, right."

"I don't like how you talk to Ma, John," Gabriel said.

"Shut up, Gabe."

Morgan asked about John's girlfriend.

"You still going with Mary Ellen?"

"We're still getting on," he said. John looked at Morgan hard. "You know, I can't figure how you can keep going to that school without girls." He paused and decided to lie down again. "It ain't natural."

"Morgan doesn't need girls. He's got God. Isn't that right, Morgan?"

"Sure, Gabe," Morgan said.

Morgan got off the bed and walked to the little window. The large oak looked harsh and barren against the freeze of winter. He thought about Nadine.

"That's right, Gabe. I've got God."

They heard their father's voice, home from work.

"Come to dinner, boys. And, Morgan, come and see your old father."

"Dinner!" Gabe shouted. He jumped from the bed, and ran down the stairs to the kitchen.

"I didn't know it was so hard on you, John. I'm sorry."

"It ain't nothin." He got off the bed. "But thanks for saying so."

"Yeah."

"Hey, you think Ma will let you go with Pa and me on Christmas Eve?"

"Don't start with me, Johnny boy. I'm still the older brother."

But John didn't join the banter. He walked from the room before Morgan finished.

"I don't know," he said. "I'll ask her again when the timing's right."

Morgan brushed the bedcover smooth and went down to the kitchen.

Mr. Sean O'Bryan observed the promptings of his paternal

instincts; he worked to provide for his family. Though muscular and straight-backed, he looked more laborer than warrior. He never caused trouble, and he had the reputation of a man whose steady pace carried him through the long, dull hours under ground. His one speed was never slow enough to bring castigation, yet neither did it speed up enough to invite promotion. He had strong fingers with short, cracked nails, permanently stained coal-dust black.

He rarely complained, neither at work nor at home. He possessed the limited intelligence of a man who knew his place and desired no other. His work gave him meaning, and his family brought him comfort. He worshipped his wife, he loved his children, and they all knew it. He enjoyed his pint, and if he could have one miracle from God to complete his life, he'd ask to play forward for one game on the Irish National Soccer Team and score the winning goal against the Brits.

When Morgan finally came to the kitchen, he kissed his father on the cheek and turned to go to the table, but his father stopped him.

"My boy," he said. He put his hands on Morgan's shoulders and smiled at him.

"It's good to see you, dad."

His father patted Morgan's shoulders and nodded.

"Are you too big now to give your Pa a hug?"

Pride and affection comforted Sean O'Bryan. He did not know that in this new land a priest in the family was ransom enough to raise their social status. He did not know that without this social-tithe he himself would remain sentenced to a life of hard labor, and perhaps his sons, and their sons. He believed America was different. He didn't know that even here the sacrifice of Abraham is the price of admission; and his wife never told him. He was a good, kind man, and he trusted, as all such men trust, the thick superstitions of hard work, justice, and salvation.

"You've grown some, boy," he said when he let go of Morgan's shoulder.

The kitchen smelled like steamy straw. In honor of Morgan's visit, Mrs. O'Bryan made corned beef with cabbage, boiled potatoes, and baked soda bread with raisins. They sat, and Mr. O'Bryan asked Morgan to say grace.

They blessed themselves, when suddenly Mrs. O'Bryan pushed her chair away from the table. She jumped onto the chair, and with one hand pointed toward the corner.

"Get it," she cried.

Mr. O'Bryan went to the corner and with quick, sure hands, he grabbed the snake.

"It's nothin, mother. Nothin but a little garter snake half asleep from the cold. When will you learn to get off that fear you ride?"

"Get it out of my house."

He went to the little storage room off the kitchen, opened the back door, and dropped the lethargic snake into the snow.

"Go and catch gophers, if you don't freeze," he said to it. "And stay out of Annie O'Bryan's kitchen."

As Mr. O'Bryan returned to his chair, he said, "It won't hurt you, Annie. It's gone now."

She sat down, her fingers knitted together on her lap.

"Sometimes I hate this place."

She spoke deliberately, the words like drum beats. Her lips pressed together so that her mouth seemed sutured. To be sure, it was rare for a snake to enter a house, but it happened, and she despised them for the bad luck they brought. By some hypnotic metaphor, they stood for all the injustices of America, its vast lands for only the rich, its poverty for only the poor.

No one spoke. A mother's fear infects debate.

After a moment, Gabriel coughed and glanced at his mother. "Father," he asked, "could you tell me why an angel can be a saint but a saint cannot be an angel? Think of St. Michael the Archangel."

The question caused his mother to look at him, named after the other great archangel.

"Ah, Gabriel, sweet child," Mr. O'Bryan said. "You always know how to make the peace, making us laugh. It's a good joke, son."

He turned to Mrs. O'Bryan, a look of question on his face.

She lifted her fork and took a small leaf of cabbage.

"There are no snakes in Ireland," she said.

"Now," Mr. O'Bryan said, "let's eat."

CHAPTER 6

IN GALETON, few parishioners missed the Christmas celebration of midnight Mass at Saint Patrick's Church. Some people arrived as early as 10:30 to visit with neighbors and to get the best seats. By 11:30, with the singing of carols, there remained standing room only.

The O'Bryan family began early to prepare. Mrs. O'Bryan insisted that Mr. O'Bryan wear his only suit, dark blue, fitting for funerals and weddings, and more uncomfortable emotionally than physically for him since he felt that such formal attire removed him from the fellowship of his peers.

Mrs. O'Bryan wore a chaste ankle-length dress, with white lace embroidered around the neckline. She brushed her long, red hair and tied a white bow at the back, creating a train of hair for accent. For head covering, she wore a white lace hair net to match the dress trim, and she pinned it to her hair in a way that left the ribbon accentuated. She knew every eye would be on Morgan and his family, and she wanted to look her best. She powdered a little blush on her cheeks; wore red lipstick, her sister, Lillian, insisted; used a small amount of eyelash extender; and clipped small, green earrings to her lobes. Finally, she adorned her finger with her other treasured inheritance, a one-half carat emerald set in yellow gold, also passed to her on her wedding day, belonging first to her grandmother, then to her mother, and now to her.

Morgan wore the white shirt, black tie, black pants, black belt, black socks, and black shoes his mother laid out for him. The pants and shoes were early Christmas presents since he had outgrown his others. He carried his cassock and his Third Order rope, both hung on a sturdy, wooden hanger, the cassock creaselessly pressed, the rope recently bleached.

At 10:15 they walked to Church. The winter air quickened their cheeks, and freshly fallen flakes of snow sparkled in the moonlight. Mrs. O'Bryan directed Mr. O'Bryan to take the younger boys ahead to settle into the front pew, and she reminded him to reserve her spot at the end, near the aisle.

Mr. O'Bryan and the boys went in, while Morgan and his mother lingered. They stood in front of the imposing statue of Saint Patrick, more than eight feet high, resting on a pedestal of rough granite. Attached to the base, an engraved plaque bespoke the ancient blessing of kingship.

To all true men of God be fair weather,
calm seas,
abundant harvests,
and fruit trees heavy laden.

The history of this gift to the parishioners continued to cause mild consternation among some parties.

When Father O'Grady decided to build a new brick church to replace the small wooden one, he announced his desire from the pulpit every Sunday for months, but the collection plate offerings increased little in spite of his enthusiasm. He managed to save several thousand dollars by frugal economic strategies like leaving the lights off during weekday Mass and by opening a thrift shop of used clothing. Since all Catholic churches must be built with cash, in the end he had to ask the Bishop for most of the money. The Bishop kept a fund for buildings, and he loaned it to the parishes at one and a half percent over prime.

Father O'Grady, in order to insure that the parishioners gave enough money to repay the loan, devised a strategy. Each week, on the back of the church bulletin, he printed the names of every family in the parish, and next to the name listed the amount each put in the collection envelope. Although this tactic did alienate a few members, generally it had the effect of rejuvenating in the parishioners the joys of tithing. Within the first three years, donations allowed Father O'Grady to pay the principal down by nearly eighteen percent, and to reward his faithful, he purchased the replica of their favorite saint and dedicated it to them.

The statue depicted the beloved prelate with his bishop's miter and royal robes. In his right hand he held his staff, and with it he pointed to a snake whose humbled belly-crawl portrayed the fact that Patrick commanded all snakes off the island. In his left hand he held the three-leafed clover with which, the legend teaches, he converted the entire green isle by pointing out its similarities to the holy trinity; as the clover has one stem and three distinct leaves, so too is God one with three distinct persons.

Morgan gazed up at the statue. He loved Patrick for his courage and his intelligence, two attributes he wished to foster in his own life.

"It's getting late," his mother said.

"Yes, mother."

They walked through the front doors and down the center aisle.

Only the lights along the outside walls burned, to save electricity. This economical gesture enhanced the dancing flames of the votive candles in front of the statue of Mary, and as Morgan looked at the statue, there in the shadowy chamber, she seemed to look back at him. The clicking of his new shoes echoed, and he wondered if the noise disturbed her.

Morgan and Mrs. O'Bryan walked past the altar-rail and into the dressing area at the side of the altar. Mrs. O'Bryan took the cassock from Morgan, placed the hanger over a hook on the door.

"Get ready," she said.

Morgan pulled his cassock from the hanger, while his mother moved the kneeler and a chair to the side of the altar. Morgan, being the only seminarian at Saint Patrick's parish, filled an unusual position within the service. He did not act as altar boy, and he could not con-celebrate, so his mother had arranged a place of honor, a small, padded kneeler and a chair alongside the altar, a position which placed Morgan in line with the priest at the consecration, and in view of the entire congregation.

He looped the rope around his waist as his mother returned. Mrs. O'Bryan straightened the rope, moving the knotted length to the exact center of Morgan's side, like the hilt of a sword. She looked him over, nodded, and left.

After his mother closed the door, he loosened the rope and pushed it to the top of his hip bones because it made him feel manly, like blue jeans pushed below his belly button.

Father O'Grady turned up the lights. The altar boys lit the main altar candles and the red Yule Candle, positioned just off the altar near the communion rail. Poinsettia plants lined the top of the altar, and the hay in the manger mixed its golden smell with the aroma of green spruce branches.

Morgan lit the charcoal in the censer, preparing for the opening procession. As soon as he added the incense and the smoky clouds of ecclesiastical solemnity swirled, he felt, suddenly and immediately, the tradition and pageantry of centuries of ceremony, the union of past to present, the God made flesh, and his own insignificant place in it all. He felt humbled as he marveled at the mystery which enclosed him with the same security, perhaps, that the infant Christ felt surrounded by the Magi and the shepherds and the milk cow. Surely, his privilege included more than a kneeler and a chair.

When the choir began to sing, and the parishioners joined in, the untrained voices blended in an odd, melodious sound, the bittersweet nostalgia of carols sung only once a year, made romantic through tradition. Silent Night. O, Little Town Of Bethlehem. Away In A Manger. Joy To The World. I Saw Three Ships. The lyrics, washed in the enchantment of musical imagery, and emanating the possibility of a realm without sickness, without hunger, prophesied by God whose creative resources offered eternal peace, bound each member to the family and each family to the clan. Once a year, the celebration in song and ceremony of the birth of the God-child dispelled the frigid fallowness of winter's equinox and gave them hope. Praise and supplication rose in their voices, and the possibilities of both comfort and reward filled them.

Kneeling at the side of the altar, Morgan felt that comfortable tranquility brought on by the monotony of repetition of the Litany of the Saints.

He closed his eyes at the consecration, that momentary instant of eternal renewal, of life over death, of Adonai.

At the Halleluiah, he sang with a lowered voice, but with the enthusiasm of high holiday, and in his heart he felt what one might consider a sensation of holiness, a spiritual sensation that lingers like the scent of mint after a spring rain.

When the Mass ended, the altar boys extinguished the candles, the parishioners honored the Christ child at the manger, and Morgan met his mother at the side of the Church. She stood next to her sister, Morgan's Aunt Lillian, and they greeted friends who passed, many of whom told Morgan how handsome he looked and asked if he would keep them in his prayers.

The O'Malley family stopped. Caroline held her mother's arm.

"Hi, Morgan," she said.

"Hello, Carol."

Aunt Lillian moved a bit to allow them to join the circle.

Mrs. O'Malley said, "Morgan, you are an inspiration, and we're blessed to have you among us."

Morgan nodded, and lowered his head so as not to seem proud.

"He's a real charmer, ain't he?" Aunt Lillian said, and Mrs. O'Bryan turned a stern eye on her sister for such a description.

"He can't help who he is," Mrs. O'Bryan said to everyone. "When someone is called, he's called, and of the Irish, the called are the most blessed." She smiled at Morgan and gestured toward him with her gloved hand. "And though he don't have my red hair, he does have my Irish blood."

With that, the O'Malleys said good night.

Mrs. O'Bryan began to walk toward their home, Lillian at her side, Morgan next to Lillian. At one-thirty in the morning, on a winter clear night sprinkled with star glimmer against frozen tree branches, the snow crunched under their shoes.

"Mother, I'd like to go with father and John," Morgan said.

"How many times will you bring that on me? Every year it's the same thing. You can't go."

"I don't understand. Why can't I?"

The tradition of visiting relatives and close friends after midnight mass included the drinking of a toast at each house. Normally, visiting lasted until sun-up, and nearly everyone endured drunkenness for the sake of tradition.

"I promise not to drink," he said.

"No."

They continued on, exhaling smoky breaths into the dull night. As they neared the deep bend of the river, Aunt Lillian hugged Morgan's arm and pulled him close to her.

"I'll tell you why you can't go," she said.

"Now, Lillian," Mrs. O'Bryan interrupted.

"Never mind, Annie. It's time he knew. Look at the size of him. He's growin up, and someone needs to explain the facts of life."

"You'll be fillin his head with wild ideas and blasphemies."

"Hush," Lillian said.

Lillian looked at Morgan directly in the eyes, not blinking. "The truth is," she said, "you make people nervous. They want to drink and swear and tell dirty jokes, but when you're around they feel like they have to behave."

Morgan looked from his aunt to his mother. The wind cut tiny red chap marks on his cheeks. He thought about what John had said, and now this. He knew he felt uncomfortable around others when he came home; he did not know he caused that feeling in them.

The center of the river had not yet frozen, and the bright moon reflected in the iron gray current, casting sparkling shards of undulating movement atop the drifting water. Across the river, multicolored Christmas lights brightened the hillside.

"It must seem puzzling," Aunt Lillian offered.

Morgan raised his head and watched the spray of exhaled air which streamed from his nose. He did not look at Lillian or at his mother; instead, he looked at his breath. He thought how it proved the life within him, a wintry confirmation of his invisible heart and lungs. But the burden of solitude flowed through him as well, deep and unstoppable.

"Yes, Aunt Lillian. It puzzles me that I hurt people."

His mother turned her head away at the words, but Lillian patted his arm.

"No, child," she said. "You do not hurt people at all. That is what you do not understand."

A sharp wind laced the surface of the water.

"What don't I understand?" he asked.

"Stop," his mother said. "He'll understand in time."

"It's time now," Lillian insisted. "We've discussed this, Annie. And you agreed."

"But you'll spoil him."

"You would protect him."

"Of course I would protect him. As any mother."

"But you cannot protect him."

"I wish you two would stop," Morgan said. "I don't like it when you fight. I don't want to know anything. I won't go visit the families. I'll just go home to bed."

He turned away from the river, but Lillian again grabbed his arm.

"Wait. Please."

Morgan stopped.

"Annie," Lillian said, "we'll come along in a minute."

"I still don't like it."

"What must be, will be."

Mrs. O'Bryan nodded, more from reluctance than from agreement. "I'll go and put on the coffee," she said. "Sean'll have the children home by now, and he'll be wanting to visit the others." She began to walk away. Over her shoulder, she said, "You two come along soon, or this night'll be the death of ya."

Lillian waited for the sound of Annie's footsteps to soften.

"Have you ever wondered why we Irish live on the west side of the river and the owners of the mines live on the east?"

"I've never thought about it," he admitted.

"It's the way of things," Lillian said. "The sun rises in the east, coming above the hill there, breaking against the river, announcing the morning. Every morning; day after day; year after year."

"I don't need a science lesson," he said.

"Don't be a wise cracker," she snapped, but small crinkles formed at her eyes. "Ah, but you are the nephew of your aunt, aren't you?"

She pointed across the water.

"You see the houses against the hillside? The trees surrounding them? They don't get the first light. While our kind is gettin ready to go to work, them across the way is still warm in their soft beds, resting so they can come later to check up on us. It's the way of things."

Morgan studied the massive hillside cuts which led to the sublime structures on the east side of the river. Even with the austere beauty of the seminary buildings as reference, he could not imagine the lush interiors of those houses.

Lillian turned back to the west and faced the simple wooden structures along the path. "These people, Morgan, your people, haven't got the safety of money and power. All we have is each other. Have you ever watched the men drag themselves home at the evening? The sun is beginning to set beyond that hill. It's dark on our side of the river so we know it's nearing time to sleep and get ready for another day. Across the way, the evening rays linger, giving the owners more time to finish their large meals and their liquored drinks from crystal glasses. Do you see, boy, what I'm aimin at?"

The Christmas night sky, filled with stars placid against the black space, calmed him. Beauty sometimes appeared in the form of nature's elements for Morgan. After all, his youth protected him from the need to distinguish between the cost of an object and the preciousness of it.

"I've never considered that God would make one day for workers and a different day for owners," he said. "But I do admit their houses are greater, and I do imagine them warmer than ours. I don't like the cold, Aunt Lillian. It hurts me sometimes."

"Yes, dear. It's a hurt everyone knows, and some will never unlearn it. That is why they honor you, Morgan. A priest in the midst of their suffering connects them to God in a way which gives them hope. And without hope, we are all doomed."

"But I'm not a priest. Maybe I'll become one, maybe not. I'm only seventeen years old. How can I know what I'll become?"

"Maybe you will, maybe you won't. It doesn't matter to them. What matters is that someone is willing to take their sorrows to the altar."

Morgan tilted his head, like a question mark.

"You see," she went on, "the roughness of their work includes more than just the labor. These poor slobs who manage to bring home barely enough to survive, they have no courage to confront the owners or demand better. They have no courage to approach the altars of power, either of this world or the one beyond. They accept their dirty fate on earth, but the God of heaven gives them hope, and they love the go-between, the priest."

"I see."

"Yes, you see. And that is why you can be one of them no longer. That is why you are excluded. You don't hurt them, child, you heal them."

"And what if I don't become a priest?"

"You will become ordinary, and they will find another."

"That's quite a fall."

"It's only a fall if you believe."

"Don't you believe?" he asked, surprised.

"No."

Morgan studied his aunt, trying to determine the integrity of her answer. She allowed him to look at her, but she did not waver. Finally, he said, "I love you, Aunt Lillian."

"What did you say?"

"You treat me like a person. It's like you know my struggle."

He felt less alone, as if at least one other person understood the contradiction contained in the phrase, holy man.

"Why did you tell me all this?"

"Because they believe."

"Where does that leave me?"

"Still alone. Actions of faith are always singular."

"You're a big help, Auntie."

"Hold that sharp tongue in place," she said. "It reminds me of your mother."

He thought perhaps she was serious.

"Come along, now. You'll be joinin your mother and me tonight."

"I will?"

Lillian winked, grabbed his arm, and together they turned against the night and walked to his home.

CHAPTER 7

AS THEY ENTERED THE HOUSE, Morgan smelled fresh coffee, a morning smell at night, like a warm day in late autumn. A small flame under the burner kept the glass pot warm. His mother sat alone at the table. His father and John had gone to visit the families. Gabriel was asleep.

The two sisters celebrated the long Christmas night with a ceremony of their own, fashioned from a lifetime of sisterly intimacy. Its present form evolved from their childhood, when, after arriving in America, they devised various methods to help each other absorb the newness of the new world.

Morgan, of course, knew of their mild predilection for holiday veniality, but never before had anyone been invited, and curiosity flooded him.

"I have a surprise for you, Morgan," Lillian said. She tapped the large pocket of her coat. "In here. Tonight I myself am introducin you to Irish whiskey." And with that she pulled a small bottle of Jameson from the pocket, placed the bottle on the table, hung her coat over the kitchen chair, and sat next to her sister.

Morgan looked at his mother, uncertain how to react. Would she really allow him to join them?

"She's a bit touched, you know. Hasn't never recovered from the convent," his mother said. "Some people can't take it. But it is Christmas, and we'll let her have her way."

She gestured toward the chair, so he removed his coat and sat down across the table from them.

An overhead light bulb burned above the kitchen table, and the iron radiator in the corner hissed. The pint of Jameson stood in the center of the table like a majorette in the middle of an empty soccer stadium. The sisters sat close to each other. Lillian rubbed her hands together and blew her breath into them, but his mother sat quietly, pensive and uneasy.

"Well?" Lillian asked, looking sideways at her sister.

"I don't think it's such a good idea."

"Don't start, Annie. Just do it now."

"Oh!" Annie's firm voice gave in.

Without looking at Morgan, she brought a pack of Lucky Strike cigarettes and a box of stick matches from the pocket of the apron she wore to protect her Christmas dress. She placed them on the table, the matchbox on top of the cigarettes neatly lined up with the outside edge of the cellophane. She held her hand above them, and might have decided to take them back, but Lillian stopped her.

"Don't you dare," she said. "Go and get an ash tray. It's time he learned all our dirty little secrets. Besides, it's only fair to him. Let him know what he's missing."

Annie went to the cupboard and reached behind the dishes to the back of the second shelf. She returned to the table and put the ash tray between the cigarettes and the whiskey.

"I don't want him to be thinking about what he's missing. I'd rather he's thinking about all he will gain."

"Gain? He's the lamb, and we both know it. Now get the coffee. I'll get the mugs."

Lillian brought three small mugs and a white porcelain bowl filled with brown sugar. Annie brought the coffee pot, a spoon, and some paper napkins. She filled the cups to about three quarters and returned the pot to the flame on the stove. Lillian unscrewed the whiskey and tipped the bottle over each steaming cup of coffee, splashing a dram into each. Annie spooned a heapingful of sugar into each cup and stirred the mixture.

The women lifted their cups and touched them together. They waited for Morgan.

"Morgan? Lift your cup, son. For Christmas cheer."

He did so and touched his cup to theirs.

"Christmas cheer," Lillian said.

"Christmas cheer," he said.

Cautiously, he sipped the coffee in tiny bits. It tasted hot and smelled oddly sweet like hot milk or warm cocoa before you taste it. The warmth spread across his stomach which muted the uneasiness there. He sipped the coffee again, and the taste of the whiskey stung his nose and his throat like soup too hot or a red pepper.

The dull, dusty walls of the room seemed firm and protective as the naked light cast a round shadow like a dark halo against the tabletop. He was home, drinking whiskey, and he felt safe.

Lillian wrapped her hands around the cup, exhaling a satisfied sigh.

"That feels good," she said.

Lillian put her cup on the table. She pushed the matches from the top of the cigarette pack with her finger and lifted the pack. She opened the cellophane, tore the foil, and tapped the package against her finger. She removed one of the cigarettes, and handed the package to Annie.

"I'm not about to fascinate your mind with make-believe," Lillian said. "It's true enough you're our lamb, but not for slaughter, child. For salvation."

She struck a match and lit the cigarette, puffing out smoke without inhaling, looking slightly cross-eyed at the red tip until she could see the cigarette was lit.

Annie lit hers.

They both displayed the uncertain eyes of non-smokers, and when they exhaled, they blew long lines of smoke toward the ceiling, looking sophisticated like first cousins to Maureen O'Hara.

"It's the girl that's the danger," his mother said, but Lillian touched her hand.

"You're goin too fast, Annie. You can't just be throwin out laws like they was fish. It's a gentle tongue that binds."

She smiled at Morgan. She lifted the pack of cigarettes toward him and offered him one.

"It's okay," she said. "You cannot make a sound judgment of a thing knowing only one half of it. True holiness don't come from innocence but from knowledge."

"Not carnal knowledge," his mother said.

"Will you back down, Annie?" Lillian said.

Returning her gaze to Morgan, she continued.

"A one track mind your mother has. It's the girl that's got her spooked. Nadine. Lovely name. Is she Irish? Not really an Irish name, but it sounds like one. No matter, I suppose. It's the fear of the common what's got your mother. Commonness is an affliction that burdens many folks, of course. Won't you take one of these cancer sticks?"

She pushed the pack of cigarettes across the table.

Morgan removed one and held it between his fingers. He had touched cigarettes before, but he could not remember ever really holding one. They were common enough, like sin, but he obeyed his mother's myth that priests don't sin no matter what form the sin takes, and cigarettes were certainly associated with sinning and sexuality, and he couldn't help feel that the pure white paper in his fingers surrounded a dark and sinister consequence. He turned it and looked at it while Aunt Lillian continued to speak.

"Commoners is what we are, Morgan," she said, "but only by the sad circumstances of birth and migration. You do have the calling, on that I agree with your ma, but I'm not one to push a boy at the priesthood. It's a holy calling, and I'm for leaving that to the Almighty. Now there ain't nothin common about the calling. It's a right powerful honor, and the family of one such who is called finds blessings on their doorstep more than they find stones. You do understand that part, don't you?"

Morgan nodded and tapped the cigarette on the table, first one end then the other, flipping it between his thumb and forefinger, looking at it, flipping it again, looking at it, flipping it again.

"Light that cigarette, boy. You're makin me nervous."

"Yes, Auntie," he replied, continuing the rhythm of turning and tapping one last time. He glanced at his mother, and he asked, "Are you sure?"

She nodded.

He put the cigarette in his mouth and held it there with his thumb and finger. Small strands of tobacco stuck to his tongue, and when he took the cigarette away from his mouth, the paper stuck to his lips. He licked his teeth and lips. The paper and tobacco rolled together, and he grabbed them with quick fingers, spitting away the uneasy feeling.

His mother shook her head, but Lillian laughed. "Wet your lips a little," she said. "Like this."

He tried it. He put the cigarette back in his mouth, and he lifted the matches from the table. When he struck the match, it flared yellow and the sulfur filled his nostrils. He inhaled, and he marveled at the sensation of color and harsh scent. He put the flame to the tip, holding the cigarette still with his left hand. He looked down his nose as he guided the flame. He drew breath through the stem of the cigarette, and the tip glowed. He blew the flame on the match with a gust of smoke. He looked at his fingers holding the cigarette, the cigarette's hot tip red and ashy. He felt initiated into a secret world. Then he coughed.

"Well," his mother said. "Are you happy?"

Lillian and Morgan both answered "Yes," and Annie smiled in spite of herself.

"My cup is empty, Annie," Lillian said. "How about yours?"

Annie lifted her cup to indicate she could stand a refill.

Lillian retrieved the coffee pot from the stove and poured a half a cup for herself and her sister. "Drink up, Morgan," she said. Holding the cigarette in one hand, he lifted the cup with his other and finished his drink. With tobacco and liquor in his blood, Morgan smiled with uneasy confidence, and Lillian poured half a cup for Morgan too and returned the pot to the stove.

Lillian grabbed the bottle of whiskey and reached across the table to Morgan's cup. "A wee drop," she said as she poured enough to raise the coffee almost to the top of the cup.

"You call that a wee drop?" Annie said. "You'll be makin an Irish drunk out of him." She grabbed the bottle from Lillian and poured another splash into Morgan's coffee. "For luck," she said.

Annie filled Lillian's and her own cup with the Jameson. They touched cups and looked at Morgan. He touched his cup to theirs.

They all drank.

"Wooo!" said Lillian, and she drank again.

Morgan placed the cigarette in the ash tray and watched the lines of smoke rise like spirits. He felt dizzy from the tobacco and the alcohol. He tried to breathe deeply to relax, and when he exhaled, puffing his cheeks and blowing from deep in his belly, the movement of air tangled the smoke tendrils. The forms floated and dispersed, mixed and re-gathered, and the performance fascinated him.

"What is it, boy?" Lillian asked him.

"A little dizzy," he said.

"You're not ill, son?" his mother asked, standing and reaching toward him.

Her gesture startled Morgan.

"I'm fine, mother. Really."

She nodded, but she glared at Lillian as she sat down.

"I don't like this," she said.

"You don't have to like it, sister. The boy is seventeen, nearly a man, and you'd be placin a burden on his back most men can't carry."

"He can," she insisted.

"Mom," Morgan interrupted them.

"What?" she snapped.

Morgan lifted his cup at his mother and his aunt. "Christmas cheer," he said.

"Yes," agreed Lillian.

Annie paused. Her blue eyes darted from Lillian to Morgan to Lillian. She blew her breath through rounded lips as if she were tired. She shook her head.

"Cheers?" Lillian asked.

The three cups touched, and three inexperienced drinkers drank, and gentle intoxication eased the tension.

Morgan began to feel giddy, and he laughed as he tried to light a new cigarette, because he couldn't get the flame to the tip.

"Stop moving your hand," Lillian said.

"It's all right, son," his mother said. "It's a talent that comes in time."

Morgan didn't like smoking. The smoke felt thick and unchewable and that contradiction made the experience unsettling. He wondered if all the smoke left his lungs. Yet he felt older, more mature, watching the smoke flow from his mouth, and he wondered if he looked like a bull when he exhaled through his nose. Life has many contradictions, he thought, and drank again, smiling at his mature thought.

In fact, he felt bold.

"Mother, why did you let me join you tonight?"

His mother jerked her head toward him. Lillian looked up. The women looked at one another. Morgan, watching them, laughed.

"What?" he asked.

"It was my idea," Lillian said.

"She thought it might help," Annie explained.

"Your mother's concerned."

"About your everlasting soul," Annie clarified.

"About your everlasting body," Lillian corrected. "She wants you to live not knowing sin. But who can do that but the Almighty Himself?"

"It's the girl that's the cause of my fears," Annie said. "It's the woman who ruined the garden. Eve adored the serpent, and ever since, there are two kinds of women, those who tempt and those who protect. I'm protecting mine. Blessed be the saints, when Saint Patrick drove the snakes from Irish soil, he drove the temptress with them. In America she runs free. She'll not have mine."

"But the girl is a child," Lillian said.

"A temptress."

"You can't know that, sister. It's the boy who must decide."

"It's God who's decided it, and I'm sayin so."

"Would you be God, sister?"

"No. But I would be His voice."

"It sounds like a curse."

"It's His commandment."

Morgan's eyes followed the women's faces, each terse and certain. He felt their anger, and he knew his own fear of it.

"What are you talking about?" he demanded, but they ignored him.

They glared at one another.

A cigarette smoldered in the green ash tray, the smoke undulating slowly like a cobra preparing to strike.

Annie stood. She looked down at her sister.

"You have no child of your own, so you can't know a mother's love, and you can't know the Lord's call regarding him."

"I think it's your own voice you're hearin," Lillian mused, almost casually.

But Annie didn't respond casually. She slapped Lillian across the cheek, and a red circle rose to the surface of her skin.

"Get out," Annie said. "Get out of my house."

Lillian pushed the chair back and stood. She continued to stare wide-eyed at her sister, astonished at her violence.

Annie pointed to the door. "Get out, and don't come back. I'll not have you draggin my house into the pit."

Morgan, as puzzled as his aunt, could not speak. Never had he seen his mother hit anyone, and the shock of her behavior toward her own sister made him doubt his drunken senses. He wanted to contain their rage, to grab hold of it and dispel it, but it was like trying to catch smoke.

Lillian took her coat from the chair and put one arm in. All the while, she did not take her eyes away from Annie. She leaned over the table to take the bottle of whiskey.

"I'll be takin this," she said.

"I guess you'll be joinin our dear father who drunk himself to an early grave, God bless his soul."

"Don't be bringin the names of the ghosts of Ireland against me, Annie O'Bryan. You're the one who's kilt-tied to them shores. It's your own sad confusion you bear, not mine."

The two sisters scowled in silent discontent. The quiet in the room made the slight hiss of the steam heater sound like hot stone when it splits.

Morgan, dizzy, stumbled, and the instant cracked. He grabbed the table for support.

"Mother. Aunt Lillian."

Annie turned abruptly and walked to the sink. She turned the faucet handle, let the water run, and turned it off. She grabbed the counter, her head bent.

Lillian turned away from Morgan. She put the bottle in her coat pocket, and stared at her sister's back. She looked as if she might speak. Instead, she made a sound, like spit, and left.

"Mother," Morgan said.

Annie turned from the counter. She walked to Morgan, sliding her feet across the floor, heavy and burdened.

"I told her it was a wrong idea, but she insisted. He must know the world, she said. Christ is the lamb, she said. Morgan is a man, she said."

His mother paused. She looked up at his face, moving her head slowly, back and forth, like a teacher frustrated with her student.

"She doesn't understand, Morgan. You cannot remain with us if you're to save us."

She turned to the table and grabbed the cigarette package. She crumpled it in her fist, and threw it in the waste basket.

"This land leaches the old world out of us. Fills some, like Lillian, with odd notions. Modern notions, she says, but those notions would bleed the mystery from our spirits. Leave us without miracle. Without hope."

She touched his cheek and walked toward her bedroom.

"There are no snakes in Ireland," she whispered.

Morgan sat clumsily in the chair, his head dizzy, his stomach churning, his mind moving so fast that nothing seemed clear. He shut his eyes against the turmoil behind them, and began to feel the swell of excess in his body, a floating sensation in his head, a force inside ready to flush the flotsam from his confusion, and from his stomach.

"Oh, no," he said.

He pushed himself from the chair, and ran with crooked legs to the bathroom.

CHAPTER 8

MORGAN STARTLED AWAKE at the sound of his father singing "When Irish Eyes Are Smiling."

His eyes burned when the dull winter sunlight struck through the window, and his lids closed instinctively. His head hurt, and his ears felt like stuffed cotton. He smelled the brined pieces of acid-coated food, some on the toilet seat, some on the floor, some on his arms. He pushed himself up to his knees and the small room began to spin. He grabbed the toilet to steady his head when his father walked in.

"Ah," he laughed. "Son of mine, worshipin at the porcelain altar." His father was still drunk, but he was a happy drunk, and he helped Morgan to his feet. "Whew," he said. "You stink to high heaven."

Morgan's tongue tasted sour. His stomach felt like petrified wood. His muscles lacked equilibrium, and as he tried to get to the sink to wash, he lunged.

"Dad," Morgan said. "Last night. . ."

His father waited.

"Mother. Aunt Lillian."

His father raised his chin, like a boxer unhappy about a low blow.

"Mother slapped Aunt Lillian."

"Don't start with that, boy," his father said. "Your mother is a saint, and I'll not have any word against her."

"It isn't that, dad." He tried to phrase it right. "I think they fought because of me."

"Your aunt is a fickle woman. Causes your mother more grief than a landlord. Filled with notions, she is. They're always fightin and makin up. Now don't take her side or soften her hard treatment against your mother." He paused a moment. Reason came hard to him, especially with drink, and more so with Annie. "You best honor your mother," he said. "Every night she's cryin her eyes out for you, asking the good Lord to give her strength." He shook his head. "No, boy, don't be sayin anything against your mother. Now clean yourself up."

He left Morgan at the sink and walked to the living room and his family.

Dizzy, Morgan fell again to the floor, leaned his head against the plastic toilet seat, and asked the infant Jesus, whose birthday he celebrated, to help him. After surviving dry heaves, he cleaned the room, showered, and walked to his bedroom without wishing anyone a Merry Christmas.

When the day to leave arrived, Mrs. O'Bryan drove him in their brown Hudson to the bus station. They sat on the dull wooden benches to wait. He rested his hands on his knees and looked away from her, his suitcase on the floor a barrier between them. When they called him to board, he grabbed the handle of the suitcase and lugged it toward the bus. She stood to the side. The rumble of the engine and the smell of diesel congested the air. He let the driver take his ticket and punch a hole in it.

The return trip to St. Francis seemed longer than usual.

SPRING

CHAPTER 9

BEFORE MORGAN LEFT HOME, he promised his mother he would not seek comfort from Nadine.

On the first Saturday in January, after Tierce, Morgan walked against the wind to Father Christopher's workshop, hoping the old priest might help him find some peace.

"Good morning, Father."

"Ah, Morgan. How was your break?"

"Okay."

Morgan picked up a hammer from the bench. The claws shone with silver sharpness. Obviously, Father Christopher had recently ground them. His fingers tightened around the handle. Father Christopher's hand was bigger than Morgan's, but he was old, and his grip frail. He had glassed the gripping section down to a thin, efficient size and then cut cross stitches in it to prevent slipping.

"It feels good," Morgan said, and he swung at invisible nails.

Father Christopher continued working at his wooden crucifix and the body of Christ he was whittling from pieces of balsa wood, one for the head, one for the torso, and two for the legs. The plastic skeleton arms and hands he bought mail order lay in their shipping box under the bench.

"I believe I'm getting closer, Morgan."

"Closer, Father?"

"To the wounds. The stigmata."

Father Christopher lifted one of the skeletal hands from the box and held it above his head. He closed one eye to inspect the bone patterns, especially at the wrist.

"Michelangelo opened cadavers to learn about the body, the lines of muscles, the size of bones. For that, he can thank the Augustinian Prior at Sancto Spirito, the wise Niccolo Bichiellini. I'm not so lucky. The human body remains a mystery to me. That's why God hasn't sent the blessing yet. But soon, Morgan. Soon."

Morgan nodded.

"You seem quiet. Anything wrong?"

"No, not really."

"Um?"

"Well, Father, it's Nadine."

Father Christopher sat in his lawn chair. He lifted a hand to invite Morgan to talk.

Morgan sat on the stool by the workbench and leaned his elbow on the bench.

"You see, Father, I promised my mother that I wouldn't see her again."

"I see." Father Christopher laughed.

"I don't see what's so funny."

Father Christopher laughed again.

"Father."

"Don't you see, boy?" And he laughed again. "There it is again, the word see."

"See?"

"Yes. We kept using the word see, and actually, I wanted to talk to you about seeing. I wasn't sure how to bring it up, but here it is."

"What does seeing have to do with Nadine?"

"I don't know. You'll have to figure that out for yourself. But it is time for you to begin some new training."

"New training?"

"God doesn't just drop in on us. There are rules, or at least guidelines. Prayer is about power, and power is about concentration. So you've got to learn to concentrate."

"Father, what are you talking about?"

"Can't you see?" he asked, and laughed again.

"It is kind of funny," Morgan grinned. "But, really, Father, what are you getting at?"

"Your calling, Morgan. The Lord has work for you to do, and you have to train."

Morgan didn't argue. He wasn't sure what God wanted from him, but he trusted the old priest.

"Concentration can be learned," Father Christopher said. "Here's how to begin. Take a walk. It's better to walk the same path every time, at least for now. So you take a walk along the same path. Begin some place and end some place, but make certain you know the beginning and the end. Got me?"

Morgan nodded.

"After you establish the path, when you begin, look at something. A stick, a leaf, a flower, a piece of bark on a tree. Something small, but specific. Got it?"

"Okay."

"Look closely at the item, an intense, focused study. Then take your walk, and think only of the object. Go over it in your mind. See it in your head. Visualize it. Concentrate on it. Once you begin the walk, follow your path, and think only of the object during the entire walk. At first you might only be able to concentrate for a few seconds. Eventually, you must be able to concentrate for long periods, minutes at first, and later for hours. But that will come."

Morgan stared at the priest.

"Do you understand?"

"Yes, Father. I understand what you're asking me to do, but I don't understand why."

"Miracles, boy. You can't manage miracles unless you get in touch with God. You can't get in touch with God unless you pray. And you can't pray unless you concentrate. Now, go and practice."

"Now?"

"Sure now. Why not now?"

"It's cold outside."

"Don't think about it."

"Don't think about it?"

"Be aware of it, like the path or the clouds, but concentrate on your object. All manner of physical disturbances will try to interfere.

If you accept that interference, you're not concentrating. Same with your mind; ideas, memories, random thoughts will all interfere. Learn to ignore them. True concentration is focusing on one thing and not focusing on millions of other possibilities. It's a choice."

"I see," Morgan said.

Father Christopher grinned. "That's it," he said. "I'll see you to the door."

He put his arm across Morgan's back and walked him across the shop floor.

"Go now."

A light winter blue softened the late morning sky, but the sunshine contained no warmth, and Morgan raised his collar.

"Whew," he said.

The cyclone fence at the tennis courts held small clumps of snow, and quick gusts blew some of the snow like puffs of heavy powder.

I wonder what Father Christopher has in mind, he thought. What does he want me to see?

He walked along the path, making the first footprints in fresh snow. He kicked his feet, and the light snow floated, as if falling afresh. He had no particular path in mind, but he did not seem surprised when he turned up the hill toward the apple orchard. The black skeleton limbs of the trees clung to the skyline like sad, brittle fingers. He noticed a few raw sections of bark where the deer had eaten, and a few hollows in the snow where they had kicked around for hidden apples. He snaked between the trees, up the hill, into the wind, following a path more in his heart than in his head, heading for their tree.

The results of his early winter pruning showed not so much as great gardening but more as effort observed in contrast to the other, unpruned trees. The branches created a circular form, like a balloon tethered to a barked spike, and the tree seemed lighter or maybe thinner within the confines of its growing space. In fact, noticing how many fewer branches remained on their tree than on the rest, he wondered if any apples would grow at all. "I'll know in the spring, I guess," he said, and he decided to concentrate on a small branch near the middle of the tree. He studied it.

What distinguishes that one? he wondered. He studied the "Y" at the branch connection, a delicate, curving point, gray, white, supple-looking. At the moment of connection, the shadow appeared black if he conceded that what he originally thought of as black was actually dark, dark gray. Yes, the stems were dark gray, and the point of connection, in the shadow, that was black.

"Got it," he said.

He began to walk. The rough skin of the bark seemed to soften as he concentrated on the image, and he marveled at the unusual feeling of control he experienced as the texture of wood changed in his mind merely by a change in the perception of his imagination. He walked the length of the orchard, and at the crest of the hill, he looked down to the stream at the back of the property, frozen, and like the land around it, covered with snow, but distinct, because of the eroded recesses of the bank through which it flowed.

Oh, he thought, I'm supposed to be visualizing the branch. I wonder how long I actually concentrated? Then the thoughts of activity took over, the walk itself, the snow, the panorama of fields, stream, and sky, and he lost sight of the original intention of learning to concentrate. He stopped walking. He considered turning back through the orchard, wishing Nadine might be there. Then he forbade that thought, and walked along the top of the hill, kicking a path, watching his boots maneuver the snow accumulation so that he felt as though he had control over nature itself. He looked far to the horizon, to the farthest hill, at the scattered packets of snow flung like random white Dali-shaped pancakes among and between branches of the trees, and he thought how the trees seemed, without their leaves, like motionless tortured people.

He thought again about his assignment, and he realized that time had passed, and he had walked and observed and imagined, but he had not concentrated.

"This is harder than I thought," he said aloud.

He continued down the hill, back toward the main building, when he noticed Peter Di Flavio walking around the corner.

"Pete," he called.

"What are you doing?" Peter asked.

"Concentrating."

"Concentrating?"

"Well, trying to concentrate. Something Father Christopher said to me."

"What for?"

"Not sure. To learn to concentrate, I guess."

"Oh."

The wind blew, and the boys twisted their heads against the sting.

"How'd you do?"

"Not so well," Morgan admitted.

"Why not?"

"Harder than I thought. He told me to pick out one thing and think only about that thing."

"What'd you pick?"

"A branch. But I could only think about it a little at a time, seconds, it felt like."

"Why couldn't you concentrate?"

"I don't know. I kept thinking about other things. You know, the trees, the snow." He paused a moment and shrugged his shoulders. "Memories, too, I guess."

The wind increased.

"Let's go inside, warm up a little," Peter said.

"Yeah."

They continued around to the side entrance, walked down the steps, and went into the lower level, near the infirmary. In the hallway, outside the refectory, the brothers kept a pot of hot water on a small electric stove for tea and cocoa. They also left two dishes, one with sugar cookies, the other with fried doughnuts which Brother Emile cooked from time to time, and next to these, a stack of paper plates.

"Cold out there," Peter said.

They removed their coats and hats, dropped them on the floor, and rubbed their hands together.

Peter made a hungry grunt as he lifted one of the small doughnuts to his mouth. "Love these things," he said, chewing at the same time.

"Think I'll have cocoa," Morgan said. He opened a packet, poured the powder in a polystyrene cup, and added hot water.

Peter made cocoa, too, and grabbed two more doughnuts. They sat on their coats, backs leaning against the wall.

"I don't know why you hang around that old coot," Peter said as he chewed.

"He's not so bad."

"Maybe. But he's crazy."

Morgan shoved Peter. "Come on," he said.

Peter's hair was cut short, like all the seminarians, but even short, it remained wavy. He had bright, mischievous eyes and a handsome face, and his good looks tempted some of their classmates toward envy. He had a nonchalant attitude which some thought bordered on arrogance, but he was Morgan's loyal friend, almost obsessively.

"You've been spending a lot of time with him since break."

"Yeah. You've been spending a lot of time with the new guy."

"Bill? Yeah. He's a pretty good guy. I think you'd like him."

"He seems okay in class."

"Yeah. He's okay."

"What's he like?"

"You know. He's got a cute sister."

"Really?"

"Yeah. She's coming up visitor's weekend. Maybe I'll check her out."

"Yeah, right."

"What's the purpose of this concentration experiment?"

"To learn stuff, I guess."

"Hey, look," Peter said. "A black ant. What's he doing here in winter?

Peter put his hand down to the floor and allowed the ant to crawl onto his palm.

"Must have heard about Brother Emile's doughnuts."

He lifted his hand up near his eyes and grabbed the ant's front leg. The little creature struggled with its other legs trying to escape.

"Leave that thing alone," Morgan said.

"What kind of memories interrupted your thoughts?" Peter asked.

"Oh, you know."

"No, I don't. Tell me."

The ant continued to struggle. Peter looked at it, not at Morgan.

"I guess things in the past. You know."

"You were thinking about Nadine, weren't you?"

"Yeah. I guess," he admitted.

"No matter," Peter said. "Hey, tell me your worst childhood memory."

"What?"

"Go ahead." As he spoke, Peter pulled one of the legs off the ant. "Look at that little guy move. He's ticked."

"You would be too if someone pulled one of your legs off," Morgan said.

"Maybe so. Go ahead, tell me your memory."

"I guess the worst memory I have is when I was in second grade. We were playing chicken, and Jimmy Nesbit was on my shoulders. We were winning everybody, and someone pulled him off of me. He fell on the ground and hit his head. He got a concussion and had to stay out of school for two weeks. When he was in the hospital they gave him shots in the tips of his fingers."

"They did not," Peter said. "How could you believe something like that?"

"They didn't?" Morgan seemed surprised.

"They don't give you shots in the fingers for a concussion. That's just something some kid made up. Man, Morgan, sometimes I don't believe you."

"Yeah. Well." It was all he could say. He had believed the truth of the shots in the fingers most of his life, not questioning it. Peter made it seem foolish. It is true that Morgan, possessed of a natural innocence, sometimes suffered from mild gullibility.

Peter pulled another leg off the ant, and the thing slowed its struggle some, perhaps perplexed, perhaps pained.

"What are you doing to that ant, Pete? Leave it alone."

"I'll tell you my memory now. But first, watch this." Peter pulled a third leg from the ant's body and placed the creature on the paper plate. "Watch it try to walk."

"That's sick."

"No it's not. It's funny. Anyhow, when I was ten years old, my parents bought me a puppy. Some little ugly thing."

"What kind?"

"I don't know. I took it to my room that night, and it whined and pissed all over my bed. Look at that ant."

The ant tried to escape, but in its mutilated state, it limped in rapid circles.

"The dog wouldn't keep quiet, so I broke its neck."

"You killed it?"

"No. I broke its neck. It died on its own."

"Pete, are you serious?"

The story seemed to fall into the category of shots in the fingers.

"Sure," Peter said. "I guess this guy has suffered enough."

With that, he crushed the ant with his thumb, stood, picked up the plate and the cup, and dropped the refuse in the garbage can.

"See you later, Morgan."

Well, Morgan thought, that conversation should give me something to concentrate on.

CHAPTER 10

WINTER IS THE LONGEST HEARTACHE; spring, proof that God exists, and spring was Morgan's favorite season. Morgan practiced concentrating, and by the time the snow began to melt and the earth began to thaw, he could stay focused for many minutes. An interesting by-product of this discipline resulted in the fact that he could read and remember more in less time, and, as a consequence, his grades improved. He practiced as he walked, sometimes concentrating on a link in the fencing around the tennis court, other times focusing on a section of tree bark. Eventually, he managed to think about a line of poetry and sometimes an idea, void of physicality, as if he were concentrating on pure spirit. Father Christopher approved.

On a sunny morning in April, he walked up the hillside to the orchard. Coiled ferns had begun to push through the dirt; dandelion shoots cracked the earth with speared leaves; and a brisk wind mingled the fragrances of mud and tulips. Although he hadn't heard from Nadine, he thought about her, especially when he came to their tree.

Father Christopher's pruning guidance began to show. From a distance, the tree stood out. Without the entanglements of excessive branches and unmanaged growth, their tree seemed thinner, yet healthier. The tiny buds looked like lime velvet.

He decided to choose a small bud on their tree to practice his concentration exercise, but as he got closer he noticed something shiny and metallic in the cushion of the large branch Nadine used as her chair.

"The trimming shears," he said.

Folded under the handle, he found a note.

Dear Morgan:

My mother insisted that I apologize for stealing your vocation, I mean your trimming shears, and I want to know if you would like to meet me Saturday afternoon. We can have a Coke and you can meet my parents. I'll be waiting.

Nadine

Morgan abandoned concentrating, and, instead, he returned the trimmers to Father Christopher's workshop.

He did not tell anyone about meeting Nadine.

On Saturday, after his work detail, Morgan slipped out the back door and around the hill, shoulders hunched like someone trying to look invisible. Nadine saw him.

She did not sit on the branch. Instead, she stood near the brutish trunk with her face lifted up to the sunshine. Spring softened the landscape with infant buds which gave the earth a feeling of newness. She looked like a part of it, part of the rebirth, part of the slender moment between childhood and womanhood, attentive and aware of it. She wore a light blouse, shorts, and white sneakers with no socks, and her long legs looked smooth like pumiced marble.

Morgan's breaths quickened when he saw her, but doubt and guilt tainted the moment as he drew near. He had rationalized the meeting by insisting that the offer to meet her parents signified a forgiveness for her theft; that unless he made things right, their ending might haunt him. He struggled to find legitimate reasons to offer his mother and Father Gale. He could argue for Christian charity or for the necessity of helping her plan her future, but he knew these reasons had nothing to do with truth. The debate ended when their eyes met.

"Hi, Morgan. I see you got the trimmers and my note."

"Yes," he said.

"How have you been?"

"Good. How about you?"

"I've been good."

"Father Christopher said it's okay that you took the trimmers. He knew you'd give them back."

"How did he know?"

"I don't know. He just knows stuff."

"He guessed. But he guessed right. Can you come over?"

"I've thought hard about it."

"Because you're mad at me?"

"Oh, no. Because I told my mother I wouldn't see you ever again."

"Why did you say a thing like that?"

"She's my mother."

"Oh. And if she told you to jump off a bridge, would you do that?"

"Sure. I guess so. Wouldn't you if your mother told you to?"

"Which bridge?"

"I don't know. A big one."

"Like the one by the mill?"

"You jump off that anyway."

They laughed.

"Let's go," Nadine said.

They walked to the end of the last row of trees. Beyond them, a few feet of untilled soil met a vivid line of mowed, green grass. This line demarcated what the students called the public land, land outside the seminary property line. The land by the orchard belonged to Nadine's parents. Their property consisted of seven acres, most of it lawn and trees, with Dutch pine along the hill-line and old, strong maples along the East slope. The city road ended at the orchard. The Shearwater home was the last on the street, and the largest.

Morgan stopped at the point of separation between the sacred and the secular.

"What?" Nadine asked.

Nadine did not comprehend his struggle, could not grasp his anxiety.

Morgan had been at Saint Francis for three years, and in his obedience to rules, had never left the property without permission. His gaze seemed fixed on something invisible, as if the boundary were fenced. He looked at the line in the landscape. He turned his head toward the seminary, and when he looked back toward Nadine, he stood ready to walk against the commandment. Physically, it required an eighteen inch stride, emotionally, much more.

Nadine saw the consternation in the tension of his jaw. She reached out and grabbed his hand. At the touch, Morgan sensed his body not as muscles and nerves, but more as oxygen or energy. The unusual vitality startled him, and his discomfort diminished. He felt connected, connected at the hands, as it were, at one with another human being. He thought the feeling might be love, but he understood as little of love as Nadine understood of cloister, and in their blissful youth, they stepped across the invisible, Nadine as nonchalant as a doe, Morgan as perplexed as an opossum struck by the daylight discovery of his shadow.

The Shearwater home lacked the grandeur and massiveness of the mine owners in Galeton. It looked like a southern house with the second story rising above the height of the hillside. The serpentine steps of the walkway leading to the double entry doors and the river-stone chimney at the gabled end hinted of comfort. Looking up from the sidewalk, counting the twenty-one steps leading to the covered porch, Morgan imagined that three houses the size of his father's might fit inside.

Mr. Shearwater owned a moderately successful, medium-sized British import car dealership. He sold Jaguars and Triumphs. Nadine drove a dark green TR2, parked on the level area in front of the three-car garage. Inside the garage, Morgan saw Mr. Shearwater's black XK120 Roadster and Mrs. Shearwater's ivory Cadillac de Ville.

Nadine noticed him looking.

"Mom likes the Cadillac. It's big, and she thinks that makes it safer. Dad and the GM dealer play golf, so he paid below wholesale for it."

The Jaguar looked like a jaguar, a sleek predator of the wild.

Morgan drove a small Ford tractor around school property when he cut the grass or moved things for Father Christopher. He did not have a driver's license.

They walked up the steps. Tufts of grass sprouted between the stones. Honeysuckle bushes grew across the front of the house, and geraniums flowered along the side of the steps. Medium-high Douglas fir and stout blue spruce trees dotted the lawn and the hillside. The vast front yard meandered, hilly and green, and Morgan thought it would take longer to mow that lawn than it took to mow the expansive lawns of the seminary.

Nadine opened the front door and walked in. Feeling a bit like he had at the property line, Morgan hesitated on the porch. Sometimes too many acts of rebellion in one day can dilute common sense, and he wondered if he should enter the confines of this house.

"Come on," Nadine said.

Again, with Nadine's encouragement, Morgan stepped across a new threshold, into the foyer, and Nadine closed the door. The foyer split at the landing. One set of steps led down to the lower level: a game room with a billiard table, a half-bath, and a hallway leading to the garage. A smaller set of three steps led up to the central area, the living room and the TV room on one level, the kitchen, dining area and bedrooms on a level one additional step up from these. From the landing, Morgan could see a large deck through a set of French doors, and a back yard with hillside pines beyond.

"Wow," he said.

Nadine led him up the steps to the kitchen. Her mother and father sat on stools around a breakfast bar, its top covered with 6X6 ginger Mexican tiles accented with mud-brown grout. He felt the softness of the plush carpet on the steps, and he admired the shine of the tiled kitchen floor, and the grandeur of the appliances impressed him.

"Mom, Dad, this is Morgan. Morgan, Patricia and Henry."

"Mr. and Mrs. Shearwater, your house is beautiful," Morgan said, and he took a seat next to Nadine.

"Thank you. Nadine said you were very polite. Would you like a soda?" Mrs. Shearwater asked.

"Sure."

Mrs. Shearwater had black hair like Nadine, but cut short, above her shoulders. She had pierced ears and wore small gold hoops which drew attention to her long neck. She looked as pampered as her home, with smooth skin, a piano player's fingers, and manicured nails.

"You're Nadine's first friend from the Church school," Mrs. Shearwater said. She placed glasses with ice in front of Morgan and Nadine.

"Oh."

"It's true," Mr. Shearwater said. "And we've lived here all her life. My father owned all this land along the road. It was part of his farm. When they sold the farm, they kept a few acres and built their home, and then they built this one for us."

"Henry's parents used to live next door," Mrs. Shearwater said.

"Yep. That's right. Until five years ago. Would that be right, Pat?" She nodded.

"Yeah, five years ago they retired to Florida. Now they're trying to get us down there. I might, too, except for Patricia."

"I love Pennsylvania," she explained. "Besides, we couldn't do that to Nadine. A move like that would disrupt her life and take her away from her friends."

"Too true," Mr. Shearwater agreed. "We wouldn't do anything to upset our pumpkin."

Mr. Shearwater had a balding head and a patch of ruby discoloration above his eyebrow. He smiled easily, but his eye contact felt rough and intrusive. He never restricted his daughter, but he inspected her friends with the same scrutiny he applied to a couple buying a car to make sure they could afford it. He appeared muscular under the sport coat, and he looked like a man who wore a hat.

"Where are you from, Morgan?" he asked.

"Galeton."

"The coal town?"

"Yes."

"I don't have much use for mics."

"Henry!" Mrs. Shearwater said.

"Nothing personal, boy. It's just that you Irish don't buy many sports cars."

"Yes, sir," Morgan said.

"That's enough, dad," Nadine said.

"Hold on," Mr. Shearwater pleaded. "It's not like I said I hate Catholics."

Nadine pushed her glass so that it clunked over the grout lines.

Mrs. Shearwater reached her hand out and touched her husband's arm. "You'll have to pardon my husband, Morgan. He's always talking business."

"It's okay."

Nadine shook her head. "Sometimes, daddy, you just don't get it."

"I just said. . ."

"We heard what you said, dear," Mrs. Shearwater said.

"Nadine," her father said. He did not raise his voice. In fact, he might have lowered it a note, but his eyes did not blink, and his jaw tensed.

"Mother, he's doing it again," Nadine said.

"Yes," she said. "Henry, stop grinding your teeth. You know how it upsets Nadine."

"Now you two are ganging up on me in front of a guest. See what I have to put up with?"

"Henry has his opinions, Morgan," Mrs. Shearwater said. "Is something wrong with your drink? Do you need more ice?"

Morgan, uncertain how to respond, held the glass, looked from Mrs. Shearwater to Mr. Shearwater, and said nothing.

The awkward silence that seeps into some conversations settled around them. Mr. Shearwater coughed, and everyone drank, each in turn, letting the sound of the glasses against tile act as noise.

Finally, Nadine jumped from her stool. "Morgan needs to get back to school now," she said.

143

"Yes," he agreed. "I should get going." He stood. "It was very nice meeting you."

He shook hands with Mr. Shearwater first, but when he shook Mrs. Shearwater's hand, she smiled as if she liked him. He smiled back.

Morgan felt uneasy because he had not finished his drink. He always finished his food so as not to waste.

As they walked outside, Nadine apologized. "I'm sorry about my father," she said.

"It's okay. It was really nice visiting. You have great parents."

"Yeah."

"I'm serious. You seem to get along so well. It's like you're not afraid to talk to them."

"Afraid of talking to my parents?" She stopped walking.

He nodded.

"I didn't know you were afraid to talk to your parents."

"I didn't say that," he said.

"Okay," Nadine said.

She looked away from him, up to the sky. The clouds moved in the wind.

Morgan looked down at his shoes.

A spotted marsh wren warbled.

"Hey," Nadine said. "Race you to the orchard."

She took off, her runner's stride graceful and strong. Morgan jumped after her. She climbed the hill with firm feet, but Morgan slipped on a muddy spot. Nadine slowed so Morgan could catch up.

"No fair," he said. "I slipped."

The shade of the trees cooled the air, and they walked in it as two friends might.

"I'm glad you came," she said.

"Me too. I wish we could spend more time together."

"Me too," she said, "but I've got to go now."

She kissed him on one cheek and touched him with her hand on the other.

Morgan watched her exit the orchard and disappear behind the hill like a sunset concluding a day, and as he turned toward Father Christopher's workshop, he thought that he might love Nadine. As he thought about it, he realized that the sensation of Nadine's lips on his cheek and the mingling of their eyes, represented aspects of the process of falling in love, and he suspected he might be ensnared in that process. He wanted to talk to someone about it, and Father Christopher seemed like the right choice. He wondered if the priest would have to report him to Father Gale; after all, they didn't allow girls into the seminary for a reason.

Perhap, he could ask for confession. Father Christopher would be bound by secrecy and he couldn't say anything to anyone. As he came to the door of the workshop, that's what Morgan decided to do.

Father Christopher stood at the bench, holding a piece of broken green glass up to the light.

"Father," Morgan said, "I must confess."

"What's wrong?" the priest asked, turning.

"I'm in love."

"Since when does love require absolution?"

"I mean I think I'm in love, and I don't know if it's a sin."

"If God is love, how can love be a sin?"

"But, Father, celibacy."

"But, Mike, love."

Morgan walked to the bench.

"I'm confused," he said.

Father Christopher held a hammer handle in front of his eyes, twisting it back and forth.

"Father," Morgan asked, "have you ever been in love?"

"That's a strange question to ask a priest."

"Have you?"

"Morgan, have you ever glassed a hammer handle? Best glass is from a Coke bottle. It's thick, and when you break it, the corners break at a thin angle like this." He held the broken glass for Morgan to look at.

"We met in Norfolk, Virginia, before I went to sea. Before the trenches."

Morgan sat down.

"She was a nun, a teacher at the Catholic school. Dedicated to her children and her calling. When she could, she visited the sick at the naval hospital. We met there."

He picked up the handle.

"A good handle is made from hickory. These days there's a lot of maple around, but the best is hickory. Holds a shape longer, and it absorbs more shock." He held the handle in front of Morgan's face. "Notice the grain; tight. Doesn't break as easy as maple, either."

Father Christopher placed the top of the handle against the bottom of the hammer head and marked the excess with a pencil. "I rough the shape on the grinder. Saves a little time."

He turned on the grinder and touched the tip of the handle to the wheel stone, turning it one way, then the other. When he finished, he turned off the grinder.

"It began with casual conversations. We drank coffee, and we talked about the sick, about the war."

He picked up the piece of glass and held it firmly in his fingers. He pulled it against the roughened end of the handle.

"I drank coffee," he corrected. "She drank green tea. Claimed cigarettes and coffee were bad for the body. But she never once made me feel guilty. Never even suggested I should quit either habit."

He continued to pull the glass against the wood, and thin, curled strands of hickory rolled in front of the glass with each effort.

"Sandpaper raises the grain, and a metal blade cuts the wood in chips or tears it off in splinters."

He studied his effort. Father Christopher's eyes looked bright when he talked about fixing things.

"Making a handle fit the hammer head takes patience, Morgan. Slow and deliberate strokes. Testing every few turns to judge the amount left to remove for a tight fit. It's like our own lives, in a way. If we let the Lord prepare us, we'll fit precisely into His will, like the handle fits into the hammer head."

He returned to the patient scrolling of the wood.

"That's why I fell in love with her, I think."

"Because she fit in God's will?"

"Because of her gentleness. I never saw her angry. Never lost her temper. She had short blond hair, straight and shiny. She removed her wimple before I left so I could see it, touch it. It smelled clean, like soap and cold river water. I can still smell her sometimes."

He pushed the handle into the hammer. The tip fit, but the fit was so precise that the handle would not fit by simply pushing it against the hammer head.

"Look," he said to Morgan. "See how tight?"

Morgan looked.

"Perfect," Father Christopher said. "Now we'll beat it in, real snug."

He took a different hammer in his right hand while he held the freshly prepared handle upside down, stuck into the bottom of the metal head. He beat on the bottom of the handle.

"Don't beat the hammer head," he said. "Hit the handle bottom like this."

He hit the bottom of the handle again, then again several times, and the head pulled itself onto the wood.

"One morning I woke up, and the only thought on my mind was Rosa. I knew I was in love with her. It surprised me, the intensity of it. I would have left the priesthood for her. I told her so, too. She said no, she would not ask such a thing."

He laughed, and it sounded like smiling at a memory out loud. The stillness of the moment held, and Father Christopher's eyes seemed to look away, into the past.

He blinked suddenly and returned to the present.

"Other lessons in a hammer, Morgan," he said.

"What kind of lessons in a hammer, Father?"

"It's a tool for our work, and when we work, just as when we live, sometimes there will be pain."

He slammed the hammer down on his big finger, and blood crept from the cuticle.

"Father!"

"It's nothing," he said. "There's another lesson."

"What's that?"

"It feels good when it stops hurting."

Father Christopher put the hammer into a pail of water.

"Got to let it soak overnight. The water will make the wood swell and expand into the metal head. Tomorrow, a perfect fit."

He put a rag around his bleeding finger and held pressure around it.

"That's the moment I carry with me because two things happened that changed me. When she held my hand in both of hers, I felt as if God had made her from my missing rib. That maybe this is how He chooses the male and the female partners. You know, like Eve from Adam. The second thing was her truthfulness. When she looked at me, she could see inside. She saw my fear. I never told anyone how afraid I was of going to the front, of dying, of cowardice. I knew I had never been fully honest with another human being, not totally, not completely. She made me see that, and it humbled me, guided me into a practice of charity I had only studied in books. She gave me the courage to face the war. She is the one I thought of when I wanted to kill myself. She reminded me that love does not behave badly. For her, I endured."

His hands were clasped as if in prayer.

"That is my love."

"And you've loved her all these years?"

"Love doesn't count years, son. Love endures. That's how you know it's real."

"Why didn't you marry her?"

"Oh, I would have."

"What happened to her?"

"She said, 'I don't want to say good-bye,' so we held one another. Minutes and minutes without a word. Then she turned from me and walked away. We never even kissed. One regret I have is that we never kissed."

Father Christopher sat in the aluminum lawn chair near the wall.

"The feeling of certainty I felt as the door closed surprised me. As if our meeting, our love, and our separation meant something to us only we could know. It put me in mind of Bach's Chaconne. He wrote it for his wife, Maria Barbara, the mother of seven of his children. Upon returning from a journey, he learned that she died while he was away.

"I thought it fitting to declare the moment with the piece, and I grabbed my violin and played that extraordinary rapture of Divine melancholia for Rosa and me."

Father Christopher sat again in memory. After a time, he looked up at Morgan.

"Father," he asked, "why don't you play your violin anymore?"

"After the war, I decided that I will play once more, but only on the occasion when Rosa and I meet again."

The air felt substantial, as if it were possible for memory and expectation to reach harmony like the hammer with its handle. The quizzical discourse of Father Christopher, and the frank confession of his love, eased the tensions Morgan felt from the emotions of the afternoon, and granted him a feeling of safety and perhaps even of comfort.

Suddenly, Morgan realized that the rag on Father Christopher's finger was full of blood.

"Father," he said, "let me look at that."

Morgan grabbed the priest's hand, unwrapped the rag, and squeezed the bleeding finger. Immediately, the blood flow stopped and coagulated along the cut.

Father Christopher's eyes widened. "Look at that," he said. He did not attempt to pull away, for the strength in Morgan's grip would not yield.

"I guess the blood made it look more serious than it is," Morgan said, and he fetched a clean, wet cloth.

"Here," he said.

Father Christopher took the cloth and wiped his hand, down and between the fingers and in the creases of the knuckles. He dropped the rag on the bench top and held his hand up to inspect the finger. The cut had already closed.

"Morgan," he said.

"Yes?"

"Have you done that before?"

"What?"

He held his finger up to inspect, as he might inspect the balance of a hammer handle.

"Stopped a cut from bleeding."

"I didn't do anything. I just held your finger."

"You have a gift."

"You think I did that?"

"No. The Lord did, but He used you."

"What does it mean?"

The old priest hesitated, obviously thinking. "Sort of like when I shook your arm . . ." but he stopped. Then he made a decision.

"You've given me something special today, and I want to give you something in return. A gift."

"A gift?"

"The gift of wind."

"The gift of wind?"

"Now that you're beginning to understand how to concentrate, it's time for a lesson in making choices about what to concentrate on."

He pulled open a drawer.

"Saint Augustine makes an interesting distinction between magic and miracle," he said, and he lifted up a black feather. "Raven's feather," he said, laying it on the bench. "In Book Eighty-Three of

The City Of God, Augustine explains that magicians perform miracles through their own private contact with devils. Christians, on the other hand, through God. One is magic; the other miracle. Did you know that?"

"No, father."

He opened another drawer, pushed some objects aside, and reached into its corner to retrieve a section of hemp cord approximately two feet long.

"Of course. Nobody reads Augustine anymore."

"Father, why are you telling me these things?"

"Lessons, what else? Life is full of lessons if you're willing to let them happen."

He placed the string on the workbench and patted the edge with his fingertips.

"Did you know that in his treatise, *De Passionibus Aeris*, Blessed Albertus Magnus provided instructions for throwing rotten sage into running water? Performed correctly, this will cause great storms to rise. In ancient Scotland, a witch brought wind by cutting a strip of plaid fabric, the longer the strip the larger the wind. After dipping one corner of the strip into water, she would beat the fabric against a blue-gray stone, chanting a croon which called the wind. But I'm going to show you an easy experiment called the Witch's Knot."

"Father Christopher," Morgan interrupted, "isn't this dangerous, flirting with Satan?"

"Only dangerous if you don't know where to find the real power. Appearances, Morgan. Lucifer, the Angel of Light, is also the Father of Lies. He can perform many of the same miracles as God. Difference is, God's miracles bless. Satan's counterfeits bring harm. You've got to learn to judge the difference by learning the true from the deceit."

"But, Father. . ."

"Watch," he said.

He lifted the cord and tied a loose knot ten inches from the end. He placed the shaft of the feather in the knot and cinched it tight, near the down, so that the silky barbs dangled against the hemp.

"Normally, a witch or a warlock would enclose the wind in three knots. The first knot causes a gentle breeze," he said, holding the cord at arm's-length. "Second knot makes the wind of a strong storm or a gale. Third one, a hurricane. We don't want to let loose a hurricane in here, do we?"

Morgan fidgeted and shifted his weight, scooting the bench against the concrete floor, which made a sound like a nail makes when it's pulled from wet wood. Uncertainty grew in his belly, and his jaw tensed. From love to Satan seemed like an incongruous leap. The damp walls of the workshop began to feel like chiseled maws closing upon him. His mouth went dry, and his tongue stuck to his palate. Often, he felt the profusion of agents in the workshop as gentle companions – sensuous dampness, a subtle movement of air, the uncanny colors of geological years muted into the stone as clouds mix with the sky and sunset. But now he cringed.

"Don't be so nervous," Father Christopher said. "Pay attention. I'm only tying one knot to make a small breeze. I say a few not so peaceful maledictions, untie the knot, snap the cord, and poof!"

The feather flapped in easy gyrations as the cord unfurled toward the floor. Suddenly, a soft wind blew along the wall, against the tools at the back of the bench, and into Morgan's face and against his eye lashes, and it made him blink. It was not a powerful sensation, and felt, in fact, much the same as the occasional cooling breeze which occurred naturally in the confines of the shop. Nevertheless, he jumped with surprise at the suddenness of it, or at the synchronization of it to Father Christopher's proclamations, and he prayed, "Lord, protect me," and he blessed himself, making the sign of the cross three times.

"Father," he asked, "was that a demon?"

"No," he said. "Only a demon's wind."

He pulled the feather from the cord and returned it to the drawer. He undid the knot and tossed the cord onto the bench. The wind stopped, leaving with a moan, like a small child's call into an indecipherable echo.

"Did you know," Father Christopher asked as he walked toward the back of the workshop, "closer to our own time, that the Kwakiutl Indians of British Columbia believe that twins are re-born salmon, transformed? These salmon-children can summon the wind by simply waving their hands. Like this."

Father Christopher spread his fingers and crossed his arms above his head and brought them down with a quick snap. Immediately, the call of a frigid northern wind broke against the walls and swirled against the stone, stopping suddenly upon reaching the old prelate.

"Wasn't that fun?" Father Christopher said. "Come on. Now for the good stuff."

Father Christopher lit a lantern and walked to the locked door which closed off the abandoned mine. The fire in the lantern cast a hazy copper glaze against the walls. He opened the padlock and slid the bolt, unlatching the door.

"We're not going in there, are we?" Morgan asked.

"It's a good place."

"But, Father, isn't that . . .?"

"Ah, yes. The tomb."

Morgan didn't believe the ghost stories about Francis Eastbrook, but he didn't want to challenge them either. The ghost stories remain fragmentary and unproven. What appears true is that sometime near the turn of the century, when Father James William Lewis first began the order, a young man from the town died while working in the old quarry. The circumstances of his death, shrouded in uncertainty, change with each telling, but the most consistent detail suggests that he fell when a loosely fastened guy-rope tied near the entrance of the quarry tunnel snapped free and a large section of slate burst loose, burying him. The boy's body was never recovered, and, for a time, he was disrespectfully referred to as the Child of the Slate. His name was Francis Eastbrook. Some say it is this very Francis Eastbrook after whom the seminary was named, and not Francis of Assisi, as Father Lewis insisted.

Father Christopher pulled the heavy door, made from three inch thick planks, and hung on rusted wrought iron hinges. They squeaked from disuse, and the sound pinched Morgan's ears.

"Father, what about the ghost?"

"Oh, is that your concern?"

"People say it's real."

"What do you think?"

"I don't know," Morgan admitted.

"Well, then, since this is a lesson in choice, I'll let you decide."

The priest lifted the lantern in front of his face and entered the shaft.

"This tunnel leads to the basin," he said. "They dug it to stay out of the weather."

His voice rumbled forward, downward, and Morgan heard his words from a distance, as if eavesdropping. He entered the black cavern as the light from the lantern diminished into swampy vapor.

According to legend, the early members of Father Lewis' order cut the stones from the ground, digging vertically, as custom demanded. However, the neurotic nature of weather in this Pennsylvania basin often triggered episodes of religious frustration, since the men could find themselves under a sunny sky in the morning, while during lunch-time prayers they might look up at a sky murky with rain. Wind, too, might whisper against soft green leaves, mellow and musical, then instantly change to a fierce bellow, snapping branches and endangering their lives.

The workshop began as the first quarry location, but the difficulty of excavation and the structural concerns of surcharge and erosion led to a decision to seek another extraction point. During the cold winter, the brothers removed some of the soft stone, and little by little, the long tunnel ensued. Eventually, they reached a sector of smooth gray slate, and that became the mine area. They encased that early area of excavation, added a door, and made a temporary tool storage area, which later became the workshop. This action created a fortuitous set of events because by moving the quarry location, the religious discovered a much better run of stone, and by digging the tunnel, the men could escape inauspicious weather patterns, and the walk through the tunnel saved them many steps in the evening when they quit work to return to the monastery for Vespers.

As Morgan turned a corner, trying to catch up to Father Christopher and the evasive flicker of lantern flame, he felt the strange presence of the cave, like the first day of autumn when the air thickens and the smell of ripened dewberries rises from the soil and the whispery, amber coolness causes shivers.

"Father Christopher," he called, anxiously, knowing from the stories that the bones of Francis Eastbrook lay nearby, crushed under the weight of slate and time. Dimly, the lantern washed the path with a glow more than a light, soft, inviting, and he followed it, fearing a misstep in the darkness. Morgan's ears perked in anticipation like a dog listening for a rabbit to start. Perhaps the entombed sensation led his body to transfer awareness from his eyes to his ears. Perhaps it was something else, some fear or some inexpressible expectation. Whatever the cause, he noticed the lack of sounds; he did not hear the shuffling, sandy-scratchy noise of Father Christopher's walk, nor did he hear the dense exhale of tunnel breeze. The chamber fell silent.

Morgan walked on, the glow of the lantern eventually more vigorous. He caught up with Father Christopher, who sat quietly on a small ledge, the light at his feet, the flame jumping in random patterns of red and shadow. In the light, Morgan noticed the textural change in the floor from chiseled smoothness and broken chips to an uneven surface of crushed aggregate.

Morgan sat down next to Father Christopher, his ears and eyes alert.

Suddenly, a cry broke the silence, an eerie, sorrowful moan in the distance.

"What's that?" Morgan demanded.

"Maybe the ghost."

"Father!"

"It's only the wind blowing against the cave face. Sometimes the wind blows across the top of the basin pond, and when it rushes past the opening, it makes that sound, like the mouth of any cave."

Morgan found little comfort in the explanation, one of those occasions when imagination reigns superior to science, when the mind in pursuit of the unknown remains uncalmed by reality.

"I want to go back," he said.

The sound of his voice trailed off, and the tunnel fell again into silence. The lantern flame bounced and burned, alternately coating the walls with mellow calm, then dancing like a sprite passing bitter shadows like ripples.

"That's where he's buried," Father Christopher said.

"Where?" Morgan asked.

"You see that pile of crushed rubble laying against the side of the hill?"

Morgan nodded.

"Under those stones, buried in slate. The Child of Slate. That's him. Maybe twenty feet down. No one knows for sure. They did not dig up the body. Simply left him there with no marker. No one knows why. But it makes a good story, doesn't it?"

"Father," Morgan said, "you shouldn't make fun of the dead."

"Why? What's the difference between them and us?" He looked at Morgan. "You believe in God?"

"Of course, Father."

"Heaven?"

"Yes."

"Hell? Angels? All that stuff?"

"Well, yes. Of course."

"Well? What's the big deal about the dead? They're the same as you and me. Only live in a different place, that's all."

Morgan paused, uncertain what to say. Uncertain, in fact, what to believe. His faith and his intellect collided. He did believe in God, thus, in angels, saints, spirits. Didn't that require him to believe in ghosts? But ghosts frightened him, as the devil frightened him, and he didn't want to meet either of them. Therefore, he didn't want to meet angels either, or God for that matter, because if he met one he figured he'd have to meet the others, and suddenly they all frightened him, and he wasn't sure he wanted to be a priest or a healer or even a witness to miracles, let alone learn to become someone who could unleash them.

"Father," he said, "I don't think I belong here."

"Nonsense. This is exactly where you belong. This is where we all belong, in a place which reminds us of our death and frightens us into life. Like Francis, we are all children of slate, stubborn and rigid, easily chipped and in constant decay; and yet, endlessly beautiful. Learn to love your blessings, son. Shout them, observe them, wrap them around you like cloth." He closed his eyes and raised his chin.

"Smell," he said. "Can you smell God?"

"Smell God?"

"Smell," the priest said firmly.

Morgan closed his eyes. He closed his mouth, too, and let his nostrils open to seek the smell of God.

"What does God smell like?" he asked.

"That's for you to decide."

"I've never thought about smelling God before."

"That's the trouble with your God. You limit Him. The true God has no limits. He smells, thinks, talks, laughs, makes miracles. All the time. That's His job. That's His desire."

Morgan closed his eyes again. The dank cave chilled his skin, and he shivered. He fidgeted along the ledge, yet the back of his thighs, scraping the stone, felt warm. He breathed in the oily kerosene smell of the lantern. He did not think he smelled God. He closed his eyes, tried to relax, and in his mind he saw Nadine.

He opened his eyes, and the flame seemed inordinately sharp, etching color into the stone along the floor, and the shadows which flickered along the ceiling reminded him of snakes and tree pitch, and he began to feel sticky. He blinked, and Father Christopher looked at him in a way which made him aware of himself, damp and muscular, yet childlike and frightened.

"Choices," Father Christopher said. "In the head, in the hands, makes no difference. All things done eventually arrive from choice."

"Father, this place frightens me."

"Nonsense, places don't frighten. Ideas do."

"But, Father, it's cold in here, and dark, and I feel uncomfortable, like we're not alone."

"Not alone, eh? Well, then, God is with us."

"Father, sometimes your priestly demeanor is questionable."

"You say? Maybe it's the other ghost you feeeel," he said, dragging the ees like the screech of a night-hunting owl.

Morgan stiffened.

"Okay," Father Christopher said. "Let's get to work."

He placed his hands on his knees and relaxed. He breathed in gently through his nose.

"You've seen the witch's wind," he said. "Now, observe the Lord's."

He breathed out slowly, and his exhale rattled the silence, like far off thunder.

The breath became a whisper and Morgan heard it, and as he heard it he felt it, and as he felt it he smelled it, and it smelled like jasmine and early blackberries. He inhaled and his spit tasted sweet at the back of his throat, and his mouth filled with sweet-tasting saliva like melted sugar cookies and chocolate milk. The breeze within the sound had fingers like a breeze of fingers, gentle and comforting. The fingers pulled at each of the hairs on his arms and his neck, and it fanned his face like a cool morning walk, and he sat, mesmerized. Like the easy exit of a ghost, the wind receded and lured him back to consciousness, to the abrupt recognition of tunnel and startled disbelief.

"Father," he said, "that's impossible."

"What is easier," the priest asked, "to open the mouth and exhale a breeze or to make a wind from words? You must have the power of faith if you wish to share in the power of miracle. Lord," he said, "show this young man wind."

Instantly, Morgan heard a noise like the crawling of a snake against wet sand, distant but clear. The sound strengthened and came closer, quickening his blood. At last, like a storm's approach, the sound of wind raced along the walls beyond the bend, and as he followed its movement with his ears, it sprang free and whipped across the crevices and protrusions of the cave, screaming with the wild shrill of a stallion, pinning him to the seat and forcing his back against the stone. The force took his breath, and the screaming power held him. Still, he did not breathe. Then, with the suddenness of death, the wind ceased. Morgan fell forward and inhaled deeply, sucking air, touching himself to confirm his body remained intact.

Father Christopher picked up the lantern and returned to the workshop.

Morgan sat, startled, yet intrigued, pondering the mix and portents of events. Laying claim to the supervision of nature fell outside the realm of his known world. Yet, how could he doubt the tradition of the great men of the Church, or Father Christopher, or his own earthly senses?

Nevertheless, this lesson brought him more puzzlement than knowledge.

He glanced back toward the workshop, and he watched the glow of the lantern disappear as Father Christopher continued around the far bend. He jumped to his feet and ran after him.

"Father," Morgan called, "was that the ghost, or God, or the wind?"

Father Christopher pushed open the door to the workshop and walked in. He turned his head and answered over his shoulder.

"Choices, Mike. It's all about choices."

"My name is Morgan, Father," he said, coming into the light.

"Yes. Of course."

CHAPTER 11

LEARNING TO MAKE WIND required a sense of community with the Divine Morgan did not possess. As he sat below the branches of the apple tree, he began to suspect that Father Christopher might be as crazy as everyone thought. Morgan knew he did not want to become that crazy, so he fought the urge to give away his will to a power unknown. Such loss of control frightened him. Where is a man, indeed, without the power of his will? The blank slate of life remains invisible to him who does not manage that inimitable, accessible, mighty free will. Doubt did not disturb Morgan in this arena. He accepted the law of domination of the earth, accepted Adam's commandment to name all things, and, thus, to control them. Morgan knew he must stay at all times in control; otherwise, what would his life become?

Yet within this depth of certainty, Morgan recalled the Gospel's reminder that Satan would rule the world until Christ's return. What of that? Who does control the world? Adam? Satan? And in this Olympic battle, where, indeed, did Morgan O'Bryan fit?

"Lord," he said, "I know You're in control, I do. But what does that mean? What does that mean to me?"

The Lord did not answer Morgan, but a soft breeze fluttered the leaves and rolled against the green fruit like the water in a quiet stream rolls around a boulder.

Morgan both feared and desired power. Power sets one apart, proclaims one's uniqueness. Doesn't everyone want power in some fashion? Whether obtained or not. Even upon the death bed, at death's rattle, frustrated that we may have gone a lifetime without it, do we not anticipate power in the beyond?

Morgan allowed some credence to the desire. Wouldn't life be good if he had just a little power, the power of wind, for instance? That would be something. That would be miraculous. Maybe that would be crazy. Yet, maybe people say Father Christopher is crazy because they're jealous, and jealousy, he knew, gestated from fear.

"That's it," he said. "They're jealous. They're afraid."

"Who's afraid?"

"Father Christopher, you startled me. I didn't hear you approach."

Father Christopher sat next to Morgan and leaned against the tree trunk.

"This is it, then?" he asked.

"What?"

"This is your tree?"

Morgan nodded.

"You seem worried, Morgan. What's wrong?"

"I can't make the wind, Father. I want to, but I don't know if I dare."

The old prelate closed his eyes.

"Why?" he asked.

"I was thinking, what if I lose my free will? Who is really in charge if I give myself over to another power?"

"What do you think?"

Morgan shifted his weight and bent his knees to change position.

"Father, how does the power change you?"

"Power comes to men in two ways, from above and from below. Evil power brings evil, to those who accept it and to those they harm. Godly power fosters goodness, and it always passes good to others."

"How do you know the difference?"

"That's easy, Mike. Good power heals, and we must give it away.

Destructive power is selfish, and we must keep it. These qualities represent the personalities of the givers of the power."

"What does that mean?"

"You ask too many questions. And they're the wrong questions. Ask yourself these two questions: Do I accept my gift? And, if so, what will I do with it?"

"I don't know. And, I don't know," Morgan said. "What do I do?"

"See that branch above us?"

"Yes."

"See that small twig at the end?"

"Yes."

"See the tiny leaf at the very end?"

"Yes."

"Blow a wind up to it. Make it move."

Morgan looked at Father Christopher.

"Concentrate on the leaf, Morgan. All your energy. All your will. Look at it. Close out all other things. Focus on that leaf, and blow a wind into the air just for that leaf."

Morgan looked at the tiny leaf, its thin, sea-green veins contrasted with the soft pea-green of the skin. He narrowed his eyes or his vision, he wasn't sure, maybe both, and he managed to remove all other sensations from his view by repulsing them as they arose until he saw only the leaf, its bulging veins, and its stem protruding from and firmly bound to the bark of its branch. He rounded his lips and blew, making a noise not unlike a soft whistle through a cloth.

"Quietly," Father Christopher said. "True power is not loud. It is focused."

Morgan blew through his lips, a controlled exhale of intention, as if blowing wind from his mouth were an act of the first order and not a necessary adjunct to inhaling. A long, quiet, focused, exhale directed to the leaf rather than at it.

The wind left his mouth, forming itself into movement, gathering itself into an intentional act in congress with an ever-expanding universe. The leaf reacted to the disturbance by floating up and down, like a single blade of grass bending under the impact of one individual raindrop.

Morgan gazed at the wind flutter of the leaf, in silent response to his objective. He felt the wind's passing in his mind at the same instant he watched the tiny leaf shudder from the tail end of the wind's passage, and he recognized that he had witnessed the consequences of his willful intent.

"Father," he said. "I did it."

"Did you?" the priest asked. "Was that your wind or nature's? Could just be a co-incidence; small wind passing at the same time you were practicing."

"Why do you say that?"

"Gifts are always a matter of faith, Morgan."

"But, Father, did I make wind or not?"

"Up to you."

"I say yes. Did I?"

"Don't know, but that's the wrong question. The correct question is: What is my gift?"

"What do you mean?"

"What are you going to do with the gift of wind?"

"I'm not sure."

"Learning to control the wind is training. It's an impractical power, unless you want to control the weather. You don't want to do that, do you?"

Morgan looked at his mentor with concern.

"Where are you going with this, Father?"

"God's great gift is healing. The world persists in a continuous state of agony. All humans seek God, but real knowledge of Him remains allusive. Some look for Him in money, power, possessions, control, but those things are tricks of the world, for they do not bring peace; they bring avarice. The world needs healers."

"Healers? You mean like curing lepers and blind men? I can't do that."

"No. You can't. But the Lord can, and he can use you to do it."

"But, Father . . ."

"But, Mike . . ."

Father Christopher stood. He put his hand on Morgan's head. The wrinkled fingers felt like soft lead, heavy with a mysterious strength Morgan could not measure.

"Healing isn't just about the body's skin or the eye's sight. It is also about hearts and forgiveness and dignity and courage. You keep practicing making wind. It'll come to you. In the small moments of focused relaxation, you will open yourself to the real power of the one God. It will come to you. You cannot force it. Practice is preparation for the real thing."

SUMMER

CHAPTER 12

MORGAN WALKED TO THE ORCHARD, listening to the birdsong and the breeze-song of late spring. He intended to practice concentration when he heard the chirping of a bird, obviously distressed. He bent his head in the direction of the sound and eased toward it. Suddenly, the sound stopped, and Morgan stopped too. He saw a small sparrow, its wings fanned, motionless. As he moved toward the bird, it seemed to shrink deeper into the grass. Morgan reached down and cradled the bird in one hand. It made no sound and settled into the pocket of Morgan's hand as into a nest, and comforted there, did not move. It did not even blink its eyes.

He checked it for blood or an injury, but he found nothing obvious.

Morgan covered the fledgling with his other hand, enclosing it as one might protect an offering.

181

"Lord," he said, "please let me help this bird. Lord, Jesus, heal this bird."

He opened his hands and threw the bird into the air. The tiny creature seemed stunned and began to drop toward the ground. Before it hit, it flapped its wings and began to fly. It struggled, but managed to control itself. It flew to a tree branch covered with leaves and tiny balls of new apples.

"All right!" Morgan shouted. "Thank you, Lord."

The bird remained on the branch as Morgan watched two adult sparrows, one flying toward and away from the tree, the other holding guard in a circular pattern. The chick pushed its wings out and followed the adults. They disappeared over the treeline.

Morgan felt miraculous. He sat at the base of the tree, and leaned against the trunk. There is power in miracle, he thought. Maybe that's what Father Christopher had in mind when he talked to me about healing.

As he thought, he heard the rustle of leaves, and when he saw Nadine approaching, he jumped up.

"Nadine," he said. "I just healed a bird."

"You did?"

"Yes. I caught this fledgling. It couldn't fly. I held it and prayed. And when I released it, it flew into that tree."

"A fledgling? Are you sure it was hurt?"

"Sure," he said. "Otherwise it would have flown away when I tried to pick him up."

"But Morgan, fledglings aren't supposed to fly away. They're too young to fly with skill. It was probably just resting when you came on it. In fact, you probably scared the thing half to death."

"Don't say that, Nadine. You have to have faith to heal, and I healed it."

"Oh, Morgan, that's why I like you. You're so cute."

"What do you mean?"

"You don't really believe you healed that bird, do you? It flew because it can. It didn't fly away from you because it didn't see its parents and was frightened. You're lucky too. Sometimes the parents will abandon a chick with human smell on it, but it's nice that you wanted to help."

"I did help it," he said, but he questioned whether he had managed a miracle or whether he had participated in a common, natural event.

The next day, Morgan found a note in the tree.

Morgan:

I'm sorry if I upset you about the bird. Sometimes I'm short tempered when I'm having my period.

Nadine

Morgan did not send a note in response to Nadine's. He did not know what to write, for he knew nothing about periods. He had no sisters; his mother never spoke of them; and Father Gale, to his knowledge, had never mentioned them. So he did not respond, and he wondered what magic it must be to possess such cycles of life.

He did not know how long a period lasted, but the next note he received made him think Nadine was still experiencing hers.

Dear Morgan:

Your hair is getting a little long. You need a haircut.

Nadine

The next time he saw her, she wore a white top with a yellow flower embroidered on the left side, just above the rise of her breast, and khaki shorts which fit tight around her stomach, but the cuffs left a round space for her legs to emerge, strong and slightly red, that pre-tanned color of late spring.

"Why do you think I need a haircut?" he asked.

She put her hand to her chin while considering the question. Her own hair, raven and brushed a hundred strokes every night, hung against her shoulder. She put her hand up to his head.

"It's getting long, and I like how you look when it's short with that little wave on top. Makes you look older."

He did not question the attention she gave him. He accepted it without wondering what secrets she brought to the safety of their grove. She did not suffer from guilt, and that helped Morgan forget his, or at least it helped him repress it. She leaned against him, and he put his arms around her and looked at her shiny hair, her lioness eyes. The late spring warmth felt like summer without humidity. A faint, receding smell of winter remained in the air, and that made the spring heat more delicious.

She looked up into his face, at the blond hair she liked cut short. He had that slightly tired look which poverty leaves on the skin, but his blue eyes felt safe to her. She leaned toward him, and they kissed.

They held the kiss for some time because they had waited for this moment and because they wanted it, no matter the consequences.

That evening, Morgan told Peter.

"You kissed her?"

"Yes," Morgan said.

He looked sheepish and proud at the same time, but Peter withheld his enthusiasm. He didn't frown, exactly, but his eyes toughened, and he pushed his lips together as if to restrain his tongue.

The next day, however, the strange reaction seemed forgotten when Morgan showed him Nadine's note.

Oh Morgan!

Our first kiss. (It made my pants wet!)

Nadine

Peter teased him. He composed an answer, and he insisted that Morgan send it.

Oh Nadine!

Our first kiss. (It made my pants swell!)

Morgan

Morgan rejected it. The statement expressed far too much sexuality for him, and when Peter left, he tore the note into small pieces. He wrote his own instead.

Nadine:

Our first kiss still lingers and makes me long for another.

Morgan

But that, he decided, sounded too literary. So he tore that up, and wrote simply:

Nadine,

Our first kiss.

Morgan

CHAPTER 13

BETWEEN THEIR JUNIOR AND SENIOR YEARS, the seminarians at St. Francis spent the summer months of July and August at a pre-novitiate at St. Alban's on the mountain lake at Prince Gallitzin State Park. The friars maintained a ninety-nine year lease on fifty acres of forest and some waterfront on the western sector of the eastern fork of the lake. If the boys decided to move on from the minor seminary of St. Francis to the major seminary of St. Paul The Humble, they would spend a novitiate period of one year and one day in cloister at St. Alban's to prepare for their further studies.

Instead of spending time at home at the end of the school year, the boys remained at the seminary through June to prepare for the retreat. Saturday nights provided the only free time of this preparatory two week period. Father Gale scheduled every minute of every day, except for a few hours on Saturday evening between 6:30 and lights out. Father Gale, recognizing the individual's need for occasional solitude, implemented this Saturday evening freedom.

As a break from routine, Father Gale arranged for a movie on these Saturday nights. They rolled the 16mm projector into the rotunda, and those who wished to watch brought folding chairs from the storage room. Father Gale made it clear he did not require attendance at the movie, provided that the time spent away from the group was spent in meditating on the sacred mysteries. He also assured everyone that he would never question an absence, although everyone knew he could carry suspicion like a clue, in case he ever needed it.

On the Saturday before he would leave for novitiate, Morgan went to the orchard to meet Nadine. Their kissing became more frequent, allowing opportunities to explore one another's bodies, and each new kiss, each new sensation of touch, brought them closer. Morgan's desire for her began to overpower other thoughts. During the hours away from her he practiced concentrating and calling the wind, but often these disciplines failed him as he succumbed to the longing which filled him.

He waited in the grass, his back against the tree trunk. Squirrels squabbled, making the soft barks squirrels make before they sleep.

The humid-soft leaves hung as if rubbed with emollient. The sun eased behind the hills, and as the blue period of dusk colored the changing sky, the placid whisper of evening settled against him. Summer promises the gift of never-ending life.

Nadine arrived.

Morgan stared at her night-streaked hair sparkling with shards of silver and her dark evening eyes, mysterious and bold.

"Morgan, you okay?"

"Yes. Why?"

"I don't know. You look funny." She sat next to him. "Did you think I wouldn't come?"

"I never think you won't come. And I always think you won't come."

"There's something very weird about you, Morgan."

"Sometimes when I miss you, it's like time stops, and I think it won't start again until I see you."

She said nothing.

"We're leaving Tuesday," he told her.

The evening brought black shadows. Above them, one small star twinkled, then, suddenly, a second. The moon appeared, but opaque, since night had not fully dominated the sky.

"I want something to remember you by since you may not come

back or you might come back different," Nadine said.

He smiled.

"I have an idea for a gift. I've been practicing. Pick an apple from our tree, and I'll get it for you."

"That's not exactly what I had in mind, Morgan."

"Go ahead," he said. "Pick out a good one."

"All right. That fat, green one on the small branch near the top. Let me see you climb up there and get that one for me."

Morgan made his lips into a circle. He blew gently, making no noise. Nadine looked at him.

"What are you doing?"

"Watch," he said.

He blew again, a steady breath, squeezed between pursed lips, extending the exhale like a long string, and it moved through the branches, causing some of the leaves to startle. The wind pushed against the branch and the apple toggled, like a mission bell ringing. The stem snapped free, and the apple tumbled, a cousin of Newton's perhaps, landing at the base of the tree with a gentle thud like a pellet of rain against a hat.

Morgan picked up the apple, twisted the stem off, and polished the skin against his shirt.

"Here," he said, and handed her the fruit.

"That's amazing."

"God's work," Morgan said.

She raised her eyebrows.

"It's not like you to make fun of God, Morgan."

"No. Really. It's one of the things Father Christopher has taught me. He says it's practice for more important work."

Nadine didn't say anything, but a puzzled uncertainty stretched the muscles of her jaw. She held the apple with both hands. Morgan sat down again next to her, and she bit into the apple. Tiny sprays exploded around her mouth and a dribble of clear juice slipped along her bottom lip.

"Mmmm," she said, and wiped her mouth. "It's good."

She chewed slowly, separating her teeth and searching the meat with her tongue.

"Want some?"

"Sure," he said.

The night enveloped them in shadow, and crickets chirped, moving from background to foreground, accumulating in their ears like water over-flowing a ledge.

She stretched toward him. She pushed her fingers under his shirt and pulled him so their bodies touched. She kissed him, and Morgan's open mouth fused with hers, and gushing juice rushed across his tongue. Teasing, she pushed some of the fruit from her mouth into his.

The breeze cooled their arms and their foreheads. They swallowed the apple meat, and Nadine took another small bite. She leaned against Morgan again and opened her mouth to share, and they kissed again, slowly, sharing apple green saliva.

Nadine dropped the apple in the grass, and she grabbed Morgan's shirtsleeve. She pulled him on top of her. Underneath him she felt like the discovery of fire.

Their bodies struggled to touch everywhere at once, gyrating, panting, straining. Nadine sat up and removed her top. She unbuttoned his shirt, and she let Morgan fumble with the clumsy buckles of her bra. She pushed him onto his back and lowered her nipples to his mouth. His movements were awkward and uncertain, but she guided him with a confidence that suggested she might possess more experience than he.

They spread their clothes on the grass to make a bed, but the gesture proved meaningless. They rolled against the earth. The musk of their sweat mingled with the smell of torn grass stalks. The energy of their love-making electrified them, startling skin, tongue, hair follicle, and heart. Morgan's hands could not touch enough of her; he grabbed her arms; he stroked her back; he squeezed her legs. Nadine dug her fingers into his back; she lunged her pelvis against him; and the soil and the grass and the fallen leaves stained their skin.

They held each other, and they did not want to let go.

"God," he said.

"Are you praying?"

"Praying?"

"You said God."

"Oh." Then he asked her, "Can you smell God?"

"He smells like green apples and sweat."

He rolled to her side, pulled her to him, thinking manhood required that he protect her. Nothing in his experience prepared him for loving Nadine, and he presumed he must love her, for at that moment no person and no thing meant as much to him as she.

CHAPTER 14

THE TWO VANS carrying students, priests, and suitcases continued along State Route #53, a two-lane road which curved through the hillsides. Eventually, they reached a spot where no sign of civilization existed except the road itself, and they turned onto a gravel drive which eased like a deer run through the trees.

As the novitiate house came into view, Morgan studied the architectural combination of rustic beauty and efficient Franciscan simplicity. The A-frame, located at the end of the drive, had solid glue-lam design, an open front with double entry doors, and thick cedar shakes on the roof. Subdued, opaque stains of brown and green helped the building blend into the surrounding woods. This main structure housed the kitchen, the refectory, the chapel, the library, and Father Superior's office. The furnace and hot water heater remained safe from the elements inside a small, insulated lean-to attached to the rear of the house; it too covered with cedar shakes. A Spreading Yew at the west side next to the chimney partially concealed the heating oil and propane tanks.

By its seclusion, the novitiate at St. Alban's protected the novices from worldly concerns. The laundry area in the workshop did have one washer and one dryer, and Father Superior kept a phone in his office for emergencies, but other than these, it possessed no extraordinary comforts or machines, no radio, television, or short wave.

Flagstone walkways led to sixteen out-buildings: one large metal building which served as the workshop, and fifteen tiny cabins used as clerical cells. Each cell had rough-sawn vertical board-and-batten siding, stained the same dark brown as the main house. Cedar shakes covered the gabled roofs, built at 12/12 pitches to handle the snow load. The Society remained a small order, and rarely were all fifteen cabins occupied.

Morgan was assigned to the third cabin up the hill behind the A-frame, about a quarter of a mile walk from the end of the driveway. He carried his suitcase up the trail to the small covered porch on which the brothers had placed a wooden rocking chair.

He went into the two-room building, and looked over the sparse furnishings: in one corner a single bed, the metal frame fitted with boxed springs and a mattress; a small crucifix hung on the wall above it; at the foot of the bed, a chair, a rectangular maple table, and a floor lamp; next to the bed, a free-standing maple closet with two doors, one side for hanging clothes, the other with four drawers and two shelves above them; in the opposite corner, a bathroom.

Knotty pine, oily and golden-yellow with age, covered the walls, and linoleum covered the floor. A small propane space heater hung from the wall next to the window.

The late afternoon sun shone through the single window, and birds filled the trees with song. The scent of pine seemed stronger than other smells, but the air tasted dusty with the deep wood acridness of undisturbed leaf and pine needle decay.

Morgan set his suitcase on the chair and sat down on the bed. He knew that to make a clear and truthful decision about his future, he must submit to this period of testing, removed from temptation and familial expectation.

Father Christopher told him to find the dark, quiet place in his mind. There, if he were patient, he would hear God's voice and know the immutable presence of God.

He closed his eyes.

"Lord, what should I do?"

He listened, hoping to hear words, focusing on the silent spot within his head, surrounded by the easy sounds of the forest and the odd clank and rattle of the others moving in and unpacking.

The body, the soul, and the intellect blended, and in that brief moment of calm, he thought he felt God. Is this the dark silence that Father Christopher told him about? Morgan trusted it might be, and he waited for God to speak.

"Is that what you do in class, sleep sitting up?"

Morgan's eyes snapped open, and the moment vanished.

"Peter."

"Long drive make you sleepy?"

"I was praying."

"You do a lot of that, Morgan."

"Well."

"I know. We are seminarians."

Peter walked into the cottage.

"What are you doing, Pete? Father Gale said no visiting each other in our rooms."

"Calm down. We just got here. Those rules don't start right away. Besides, what do you think he's afraid of?"

"Afraid of? I don't think he's afraid of anything. I think we're supposed to respect one another's privacy and practice the rule of silence. We all need to pray and focus."

Peter lifted Morgan's unopened suitcase from the chair, set it on the floor, turned the seat of the chair toward the bed, and sat down.

"You're taking this thing seriously, aren't you?"

"I've got to, Pete. I've got to make a decision, and I want it to be the right one."

"Nadine?"

"I'd rather not talk about it. I figure if I stay quiet, I'm more likely to hear from God."

"You don't think He's really going to talk to you?"

"Well, yeah. I want Him to."

"Morgan, if you tell anyone God is talking to you, Gale will haul you off to a nut house. God doesn't talk to people. Not anymore."

"That's not the kind of God I can believe in. I need a God I can talk to. Otherwise, what's the purpose of having one?"

"I don't know, Morgan. Sounds like you're getting as nutty as Father C."

The dusk of the forest settled quickly, and the damp shadows of night emerged.

Peter turned on the lamp.

"Man, it got dark fast," he said. "I better go."

"Yeah."

"Lighten up, Morgan. Something'll happen."

"Yeah. Something'll happen. It always does."

"Right," Peter said, and the door closed quietly as he left.

Morgan, perplexed and anxious, got up from the bed, unpacked, and organized his belongings in the closet. He hung his cassock, pants, and shirts on hangers. He draped his third order cord on a nail on the back of the door and put his dress shoes on the floor of the closet. He placed underclothes and socks in one drawer and his work clothes in another. His toothbrush, toothpaste, and other toiletries went on the first shelf, and his razor, blades, and shaving cream on the second.

He did not need to shave every day, but Father Gale insisted that as the facial hairs became noticeable, he must shave. He liked the idea of shaving; it made him feel older. But he didn't like the practice of it because sometimes he cut himself, and the little nicks bled for a long time.

As night thickened, he peered out the window. He could see the small porch lights of two nearby bungalows. He couldn't see much of the sky through the branches of the trees, but some of the limbs looked silvery, and he guessed that the moon must be high and the sky clear.

Father Gale made the first night free so that everyone could unpack and get settled. The brothers prepared cold cuts, bread, and fruits on a table, cafeteria style, but Morgan wasn't hungry. Peter's visit bothered him. He knew that friendship required patience and forgiveness, but it seemed to Morgan that Peter hadn't really listened to him. He might need to keep away from Peter. Morgan had to find his answers alone.

CHAPTER 15

THE DAYS TURNED QUICKLY to routine. Hours of prayer and reading in the morning. Lunch and one hour of free time to talk and walk among the trees or along the lake shore. Work from two o'clock to five o'clock. Dinner at 6:30. Unless Father Gale ordered otherwise, silence remained in effect. Generally, this discipline allowed speech only from necessity, say for work or confession, and then only in subdued tones.

Everyone worked. These monastics believed in a corollary to the adage that an idle mind is the devil's workshop; it went: idle hands make an idle mind. The novitiate stressed this emphasis on the dignity of labor, and since communism provided a practical necessity for the order, each individual acted to support the group by performing a specific task.

Morgan made sandals.

Perhaps because of his training with Father Christopher, perhaps because of a natural affinity to needful craft, perhaps because of some supernatural blending of these two possibilities, Morgan, within two weeks, learned to make passable sandals. Naturally, he made simple designs. Nevertheless, they fit well, left foot and right foot weighed equally, and, most important, the seams stayed together. This last achievement impressed even Father Superior, who, having watched many men attempt sandal-making, could tell immediately whether they had the gift or not by pulling at the seams.

Morgan's seams held.

The sandal-making area, located in the far corner of the workshop, allowed him a certain isolation. Angled from the corner, the cobbler's bench faced the interior expanse of the building, and he could look up and watch others come and go.

On the wall behind the bench, he hung a picture of Saint Crispinus, the sinewy, sharp-eyed patron saint of leather workers. An artist and a man of God, his facility with leather inspired cobblers with the same acumen that Aquinas's work with words inspired thinkers. Looking at Crispinus' intense eyes and panther-quick hands encouraged Morgan to concentrate on the work, as Father Christopher had taught him.

Two sturdy corner shelves hung near his workbench. Morgan placed his tools along the longer of the shelves. Standard tools, mostly, two leather trimming knives, one straight, one curved, four various-sized punches, an awl, pliers, an edge beveller, and an old leather shave. On the upper shelf, Morgan kept the rolls of shoe leather, all dyed brown, but of various shades because the brothers bought end runs to save money.

He adjusted his workbench so that he could swivel on his stool to reach the tools or a new piece of leather. He kept two mallets at his bench, one small, one medium, both with rawhide heads, and one snub-nosed shoe-maker's hammer for setting nails. A standard, two-pound anvil and a last were bolted to the end of the workbench, and a rubber pounding mat covered the assembly area. Under the picture of Saint Crispinus, a series of smaller shelves held the cut leather, thick slices for the soles and thin strips to make straps.

And Morgan found peace in the work for a few hours each day.

"You're getting quite a reputation."

"Pete."

They both stared at the skin on Morgan's bench.

"Mind doing a little repair on mine?"

"What's the problem?"

"Scrapes across the top. Here, where the strap is."

"Sure. Let me see."

Morgan felt the inside edge of the strap.

"Yeah, it's a little rough. I can trim it and sand it. Put it on. Let me see where it's rubbing."

Peter put the sandal back on his foot, and Morgan bent down and touched his finger along the strap to feel where the leather rubbed.

"It feels pretty good, Pete. I can sand it, but maybe you just need to let it stretch."

"No. It hurts. Right there." He pointed to the top of his foot. "Do something."

"Okay," Morgan said. " I'll take a little off there."

He sat down and sanded the inside of the straps. Then he took the curved trimming knife and trimmed a thin string from the area at the top of Peter's foot. He rounded the edge of the leather with the sanding strip. He felt the underside with his forefinger. It felt smooth and soft.

"There. That should help."

He handed Peter the sandal.

"Thanks, Morgan." He slipped the sandal on his foot.

"You're welcome."

"We haven't had a lot of time together here."

"Yeah."

"You avoiding me?"

"Pete."

"Hey. I'm just asking. I mean for a seminarian type you seem to be spending a lot of energy thinking about one N-A-D-I-N-E, and not so much about anyone else. You trying to make me jealous?"

Morgan did not respond. Jealousy in close communities can be dangerous, even as a joke.

"Hey, I'm here for you," Peter said.

"Yeah."

CHAPTER 16

THE DAYS AND WEEKS PASSED, and the end of August drew near. Morgan grew accustomed to the coolness of nighttime mountain air. He left the window open a few inches. It invited sleep. Outside, the frenzy of insect procreation filtered through the screen, the hum of dragon fly wings, the buzz of mosquitoes, the incessant rattle of crickets. Mountain moths circled the globe of the porch light, and their powdery wings banged against the building making a sound like wet felt.

Morgan listened, no closer to an understanding of God's mind than when he first arrived.

He exhaled an exasperated wish for wisdom and prepared for sleep. He wore only underclothes. The bleached linen sheet prickled his skin. He raised the sheet with both hands and watched the air fluff it like a breath, and as it settled against him, he enjoyed the lightness of its feeling. It seemed like a good night for prayer, but the bustle of summer sounds struck him like the curious conversation of a foreign stranger, and he could not concentrate.

In spite of his efforts, the memory of Nadine often overwhelmed him, and he began to conclude his feelings for her would control the rest of his life.

Suddenly, the door pushed open, and a brief arrow of light struck his eyes.

"It's me," Peter whispered as he clicked the door shut with both hands to muffle the call of the latch.

"What are you doing, Pete? Is anything wrong?"

"I can't sleep. I'm worried about you."

"Worried about me?"

Peter pulled the chair to the side of the bed.

"Can I sit down?"

Peter wore no shirt, only white briefs and his sandals.

"I watched you at Vespers tonight. You looked sick. Not sick. Worried. It's not like you to stare off into space at prayers."

Morgan turned his face away from Peter and stared at the ceiling.

"I hate to see you like this, Morgan. I want to help."

"Thanks, Pete. Really. But there's nothing you can do. I've got to figure this out for myself."

Peter jumped the chair along the floor, positioning it closer to the bed so he could put his feet on the mattress. He leaned over, kicked his sandals to the floor, and crossed his ankles, his feet pointing toward Morgan's knees.

"I figure you just can't get past the idea of Nadine."

"Could be, I guess. I think I love her. If I do, I can't stay in the seminary. I've got to marry her."

"How does she feel about that?"

"I don't know. We haven't really talked about it. But I think she loves me."

"Isn't it funny?"

"What?"

"How odd language is. I mean, we've got hundreds of words to describe things. Take cars, for instance. We can name a sedan, a sports car, a station wagon, a Chevy, a Ford, six cylinders, eight cylinders, one barrel, two barrel, four barrel. Geez, we've got hundreds of words to describe a car. But emotions, feelings, like love – one word."

"I never thought of that."

"The Eskimos have seventy or eighty words for snow. Us, we

got one word for love, and don't you think there's a lot of different kinds of love?"

"I guess."

"Love of mother. Love for mother. Brother. Friend. All loves, right? If that's so, Morgan, no wonder you're having a tough time trying to understand what you feel."

The night breeze came through the screen at the window. Morgan pushed the sheet off his torso. The rush of air felt silky and cool.

Peter continued. "Answer me this. Is the feeling you have for God the same as the feeling you have for Nadine?"

"I don't know. Yes. No. I don't know."

"That's my point. Yet we only have that one word to try to explain all our feelings."

Peter lifted his feet off the bed, put them on the floor, and leaned toward Morgan.

"If you can't even name everything you feel, how can you know the difference between real and fake feelings?"

The reflected light, gray and muted, glistened on his forehead and caused his eyes to appear dense and penetrating.

"Morgan, we're friends. Isn't that love, too?"

"Sure."

"Then I want to tell you there's only one way to know one love from another."

"What's that?"

"Experience. How can you know the truth about love if you only know half of it?"

Peter got off the chair and knelt beside the bed. He took Morgan's hand in his.

"Morgan, I love you."

"I know, Pete, and I appreciate you trying to help" he said. "I love you, too. Friends have a special kind of love."

"We're still stuck with that one word," Peter laughed, and he stroked Morgan's arm.

"What are you doing?"

"Look, Morgan, love is physical. At least between people. With God, it's spiritual. That's why we have prayers. But prayers don't express love between people. God gave sex to people."

Morgan pulled away, inching into the wall.

"Morgan, you owe it to yourself and to Nadine and to God to make the right decision, and you can't do that unless you compare experiences."

He stood and pulled the sheet off Morgan's legs and flopped it over the end of the bed. He pulled his underpants down and pushed them aside with his toe.

"Look at me, Morgan. God has made all of us beautiful, and He wants you to know both sides of love. That's the only way you can make a valid decision about Nadine."

"I don't know, Pete. I'm not interested in sex with you."

"How do you know? You say you love me, and sex expresses love. You can't leave the most important decision of your life to chance. Test all the hypotheses, Morgan. It's the only way."

Peter lay down next to Morgan.

"I know you're nervous. Trust me."

He put his fingers inside the elastic of Morgan's jockeys and pushed his hand under the fabric.

Morgan, astonished and uncertain, argued with himself – if any lesson were the hallmark of his education it must be to check all hypotheses. He wanted to know what to do, and correct action can only follow appropriate investigation. Peter was his friend and he trusted him, but he felt no sexual desire for him. Yet the idea tempted him with a strange and powerful repulsiveness.

He could not move.

"Roll over," Peter said. "It'll be all right."

Morgan's shorts clung to his knees, his penis shriveled, his stomach knotted, but Peter's hands pushed his shoulders, and Morgan rolled onto his stomach. He wanted to believe Peter, and he closed his eyes as he shoved his face into the pillow, crushing the pillowcase and searching inside his closed eyes for some clarity. He found none. Instead, a debris of blinking colors bombarded the emptiness, and he felt his soul go hollow.

Peter attempted to open Morgan's rectum with a finger, but Morgan stiffened.

"No, Peter. No," he said.

Peter held Morgan with his arm across the back of his neck.

"Okay. Okay," he panted, his breaths quick and sharp.

Morgan felt the violent actions of Peter's hips against his legs and the unthinkable massage of Peter's genitals against the crease of his buttocks.

Peter made a gut sound, and Morgan felt the wet sperm pool in the small of his back like a milky dagger, and he felt shame prickle him like the heat from Peter's skin.

"Morgan . . ."

Morgan, disgraced and betrayed, twisted himself to force Peter off his body, and he pulled the sides of the pillow harder against his face. He felt Peter crawl off the bed with a mild spring at the mattress edge. He listened to Peter shuffle to the door. When he heard the latch close, it sounded like the harsh reverberation of a judge's gavel.

He could not sleep. He tried to wash his body and his guilt in the shower, but both lingered, and he lay awake all night unable to quiet his restless confusion.

The devil's eye of morning, like an accusing finger, spiked through the window, and he thanked God for daylight, but he immediately took it back because he knew God would not speak to him this day. The morning ritual of cleansing felt mechanical and, in spirit, hypocritical, for he still felt dirty, and he discovered shame at his nakedness. As he dressed, he turned toward the door with every sound, expecting to find an accusation.

At morning prayers, he sought atonement, but guilt and anger merged like hydrogen and sulfide, and he covered his face with both hands to hide the stinking shame. He tried to ask God to take away what had happened, but he felt like a salmon whose time had come to swim upstream.

He skipped breakfast and lunch. He ignored Peter. He pounded at some leather but accomplished nothing, and the day formed slowly like water to ice.

Finally, he decided to confess.

Normally, Father Christopher sat in the confessional from three to four every day. He waited until almost four o'clock, hoping that Father Christopher might have time to talk.

He walked to the chapel. Mercifully, no one waited, so he opened the door to the confessional box and knelt. The priest slid the privacy door away from the screen. Morgan made the sign of the cross.

"Bless me, Father, for I have sinned. It has been four days since my last confession."

He paused. He shifted his weight from one knee to the other.

"Father." He clenched his teeth.

"It's all right, son. Take your time."

"Father Gale?"

"Yes?"

"What are you doing here? Where's Father Christopher?"

"He took a walk and hasn't returned. I'm sitting in for him. Calm down, Morgan."

"But, Father, I . . . "

Father Gale let him fidget, and Morgan tried to decide what to do. He could say he had nothing to confess, that he just needed the indulgences, but that would be a lie, and a lie in confession was like another hot coal on his chair in hell.

"What is your burden, Morgan?" Father Gale's voice sounded compassionate.

"It's hard, Father."

"All right. Take your time."

Morgan knew that in spite of his idiosyncrasies, Father Gale was a good confessor. Many of the students went to him, yet Morgan wondered if Father Gale had ever forgiven a confession like the one he was about to hear.

He told the priest what happened between him and Peter Di Flavio. During the telling, Father Gale limited his comments to "I see," and "Is there more?" Finally, Morgan finished.

"Is that all?"

"Yes, Father."

"Are you sure?"

"Yes, Father."

"Morgan from what you've told me, I don't think you committed any sin."

"But, Father . . ."

"Unless you felt desire or delight."

"I don't think so. Peter is my friend, and I thought if I said no I would sin. Yet, complicity is a sin too, so because I didn't stop him, didn't I imply yes? Also a sin. It feels like I sinned, no matter what."

"The occasion of sin and the act of sin are separate occurrences, and we will let God judge intention. What you have is an irrational distortion of an infantile wish, but let's not mix psychology with theology."

"Let's not."

"All right, then. Ego te absolvo. What sins you committed and what sins you think you committed are forgiven. Go in peace."

"Thank you, Father."

Neither spoke for a moment.

"Father?"

"Yes?"

"My penance?"

"Sometimes, Morgan, admission contains contrition, and the act itself cleanses. Go in peace."

He did not sleep that night despite the penitential cleansing. The weight of shame covered him like the resolute lid of a tomb. Throughout the endless night, he suffered the torments of self-castigation, a pitiless telling and re-telling of events which concluded with him first as victim, then as sinner. Now, how could he ever expect to know God. Meekly and desperately he hoped that Father Gale's profession of absolution would hold.

At sunrise, energetic birdsong foretold of a new day. But Morgan's skin felt pasty from sweat, and his nauseated stomach rumbled. He washed. The water felt cool, and he drank some to lessen the burning in his throat. He dressed and went to chapel, but he did not pray. The anger he felt at himself and at Peter spread to God, and his thoughts turned dark.

He noticed Peter did not attend chapel; neither did he appear at breakfast.

Morgan sat at the breakfast table, avoiding eye contact with the others. Certainly, he thought, everyone knew what happened, and they were all secretly staring at him. He passed the bowl of scrambled eggs without taking any. He took a deep drink of orange juice. He bit a corner of corn bread, but it felt dry. He wanted milk.

As he poured a glass, Father Gale astonished him and rang the small bell to break night silence. So unusual was this gesture that several seconds elapsed before anyone spoke. First one, then another, then another until the noise of group-talk took hold. He heard no words, just the sound of human voices as background.

Morgan looked up to the Master's table, but Father Gale paid no special attention to him. He simply sat back in his chair, his large stomach a resting spot for his hands. A cup of coffee steamed, and Father Gale blew across the top as he lifted it.

Morgan watched him, puzzled but curious, and it took a moment for him to recognize that the other students at his table were talking to him.

"Morgan, what do you think?"

"About what?"

"What are you doing, Morgan, thinking about making sandals? Anyway, I heard he's gone for good."

"Who's gone for good?"

"Peter Di Flavio. Geez, Morgan, pay attention."

"I heard he swore at Gale."

"Me too, but at the end of the fight."

"What fight?" Morgan asked.

The others shook their heads and continued the debate.

"Well, I heard he swung at Gale, and when he missed, he jumped over the desk and actually hit him."

"No."

"I bet it's true. It always felt like violence waited just below the surface with him. What do you say, Morgan, you knew him best. Did he seem like a violent person to you?"

"Peter's gone?" Morgan asked.

"Morgan, try to keep up."

Morgan stopped listening. He looked at Father Gale, but he finished his coffee, pushed his chair from the table, and left the refectory with no hint of explanation one way or another. Then Morgan's tablemates left, and he sat alone.

The Lord's sword is swift, he thought.

He looked up at the ceiling searching for heaven.

"What will You do with me?" he asked.

Three days later, they returned to Saint Francis, and Morgan left a note for Nadine asking her to meet him.

FALL

CHAPTER 17

EARLY IN SEPTEMBER fall arrived, the season of culmination. The days grew less humid, and the air filled with the hot dust of harvest. In the fields, acres of purple grackles following the tractors undulated like black waves across a field of blue-gray sky. That evening, a gold sunset crowned the hills, and the robins held their long notes against an on-coming chill.

Morgan found no pleasure in the sky's display nor in the birds' lament. He felt betrayed by Peter. The more he thought about it, the more guilt and anger assaulted him, and he feared that Nadine might reject him. He told her about the rape and asked her if she hated him because of it.

She surprised him.

"You call that rape?" she cried. "I'll tell you what rape is. Rape is when you're eleven years old and you go to visit your auntie and uncle on their farm and your two cousins who are fourteen and fifteen years old and who you loved and who you thought loved you take you out to the horse barn and hold you down and pull your pants off and take you and say they'll beat you up if you tell and they do that again and again and threaten you and you sleep in fear and you hate them and you hate everyone because no one helps you and you're helpless and frightened and alone and they hurt you anyway."

Her rage held back the terror, but not the tears.

Morgan reached for her, touched her shoulder, but she shrank away. "No!" she said.

He tried to talk, but what could he say? Images rushed about in his head, turning memory to anguish and empathy to horror. Peter's sensual back mixed with the image of Nadine, young, thin, helpless – and the two pictures became at once harsh and beautiful like the stench of manure mixed with the aroma of hay. He saw the harsh farm boys, strong-handed and cruel, towering over her like storm clouds, oppressive and unassailable. His own molester, gentle, a friend, but nonetheless a towering power making him mute and as helpless as Nadine.

She looked at him with eyes red and terrible, and his skin went numb and his mouth dry. He wanted consolation, and he wanted to console her, but the insanity of brutality separated them. He raised his hands toward her in supplication as much as in question. She dropped her hands to her side and lowered her head, both of them depleted from the truth.

"I'm sorry," she whispered. "I've never told anyone. I hate you that you could tell. But now you know and you will hate me."

"I do not hate you."

"What then?"

"I know you better."

"You know nothing."

"I know guilt."

"I am not guilty," she insisted. "They are. All of them."

He looked at her in silence.

"I suffered. Long nights when I couldn't sleep. Weeks and months later, fear and shame separated me from others. My mother sensed something. But I could not tell her. How could I tell her that her sister's lovely sons raped me?"

Her eyes looked both sad and furious.

"Their threats kept me silent. I never returned to the farm, but I see them every year at reunion. They both hug me and smile with fearsome eyes. Finally, on my fifteenth birthday, I walked out of school. The secretary called to me from her desk behind the counter, but I ignored her. I walked past the school busses and across the lawn. I heard the principal running out the doors, calling me. By then I was near the road, and I stepped off the curb into the traffic.

"I watched a white utility truck come toward me. I closed my eyes and waited. But the driver slammed on his brakes, and the principal grabbed me, and no one understood."

Nadine paced, the soft soles of her sneakers creasing the decaying autumn grasses. She stopped and pulled a leaf from a branch. She looked at it tenderly. Then she tore the leaf in half along the stem and threw both pieces to the ground.

"My mother bought me new clothes and scolded the principal for making me study so hard. 'Nadine is under too much stress,' she told him. The rest of that year I had no homework. That summer, though, I began to think God had saved me, that it was time to tell someone, so I went to my father's office at his dealership."

She turned toward her home and pointed.

"You like my car, don't you? Everyone likes my car."

She stared at the green Triumph.

"When I arrived at his office, some people were signing papers, so I waited. He saw me and came out. 'I've got business, Nadine. What do you want?' I told him I needed to talk, so he brought me into the second office and closed the door. 'What is it?' he asked. I sat down, frightened, but glad at last to tell someone. 'Dad, something happened. Something bad. Years ago.' I began to feel safe, that I might be free. 'I knew you were awake,' he said. 'And I knew this day would come. Now don't do anything rash. Just wait a minute. Let me finish this sale. I'll be right back.'"

She sat, and Morgan sat next to her.

"It didn't take him long. I could see the buyers were surprised by his curtness. But he rushed them off with a big smile and a hand shake. When he came back, he sat behind the desk. 'Now,' he said. 'Let's talk.' I said to him, 'Dad, something sexual happened. Something bad, and I've got to tell someone.'

"He nodded and rubbed his forehead. 'Nadine, honey, say no more. You kept quiet all these years, and I know you'll keep quiet now. That secretary doesn't work here anymore, and I swear it's the only time I was unfaithful to your mother.' He smiled at me, tenderly almost. Then he said, 'I knew you were awake, and it was a dumb thing to bring her home, but you've kept the secret well, and it would just kill your mother if she found out now, this late. Let sleeping dogs lie, eh?'

"What could I do? What could I say? How could I trust him after that? I began to cry. 'Now, now, honey,' he said. 'Don't cry. You've done the right thing coming to me, and I'll tell you why.' 'Why?' I asked him. 'Because I've got a surprise for you. A reward. Come and look.'

"He took me to the shop area. The detailers had just finished buffing the Triumph. It shone like an emerald in that dingy shop light. My father walked over to it and removed the keys from the ignition. He put the keys in my hand. 'Now, honey, you keep our little secret, and this baby is yours. And in a few months, when you get your license, you can set the world on fire.'

"He kissed me on the head. 'That's my girl,' he said, and went back to his office."

She looked away, toward the car parked like a trophy on the concrete driveway.

"Everyone thinks that's my reward for doing well in school after I tried to kill myself. But it's not. It's my guilt machine, and I hate it. And my father. And all men."

Her eyes flashed with bitter anger.

"Even me?" Morgan asked.

"You're the only man I've ever trusted. Now you're the only man

I've ever told, and that makes you just like every other man. You have reason to judge."

"No," he insisted. "I'm the one you trusted."

"No," she whispered. "You're the one I told."

"What does that make me?"

"I don't know."

He wanted their shared secrets to bind them, and he wanted to save her.

Above them, star patterns appeared – the North Star, the Big Dipper, and directly above them, Venus. To the south, the moon rose, high and frosty white.

"We see each other more clearly now," Morgan said.

Nadine looked at him. "I'm ashamed," she said.

"But it's the shame of a child who didn't understand. I felt shame, too. But I . . . I implied permission with my silence, but you . . ."

"Exactly!" she said. "That is why you will never look at me the same way again."

"You're right. I love you even more."

"I wish that were true. Sometimes I feel the weight of the devil on my back, and I'm afraid. I'm afraid of everything. I'm afraid to have children. How could I bring a little girl into this world knowing what could happen to her?"

"I will take care of you both," Morgan said.

"My good priest," she said.

He winced, and the reality of their differences appeared like sunrise.

For a time, they sat, wordless.

Finally, Morgan asked, "Can I hold you, Nadine?"

"Sure," she said, and as if toggled, her old personality returned, courageous and adventuresome.

"Such a quick change," Morgan noted.

"I've been at it awhile."

She let him hold her, and she felt solid, firm, like her old self, but Morgan knew her more deeply, more intimately somehow, and, he believed he understood her.

Suddenly, he said, "Father Christopher told me the mind, the body, and the spirit are one; that if I try to separate them I would not only disconnect from myself, I would disconnect from others."

"What did he mean by that?"

"I'm not sure, but I think it has something to do with us."

"What?"

"I think you are a part of me. That without you I am incomplete. That somehow you will always be a part of me no matter what."

The orchard shadows surrounded them with the inviting seclusion of those short, honest minutes between dusk and night which can bring people together like no other time.

"You're a part of me, too, Morgan," she said. "But now, things are different."

A breeze rustled the leaves. She looked at the sound and exhaled a tired breath.

"You've changed," she said. "Look how muscular your arms are." She rubbed his arm and the back of his hand. "Look at the veins, all popped up."

"I love you, Nadine."

"I know."

In the dark of that somber moment her eyes seemed older. A furtive twitching of her neck muscles made her appear nervous, moody and introspective.

They held hands under the moon, wrapped in the cocoon of the orchard and the smell of over-ripe apples. Intimacy entangled them, like the desire for life, unbearable and patient. It grew from the shock and embarrassment of a confession driven not by sin but by a silence of hopelessness given voice. The intimacy gave way to the surrender which binds two bruised hearts in a momentary recognition of shared human frailty. They cried without tears.

He felt the heat of her cheek against his neck. He held her head and rocked her gently.

She groaned, comforted by their closeness.

"Nadine," he said, "I'm going to leave the seminary."

She opened her eyes and turned her head to look at him, but said nothing.

CHAPTER 18

MORGAN NEEDED TO TELL Father Christopher of his decision, and the next day he went to the shop. Father Christopher sat on the stool at the workbench turning a hammer from one side to the other, studying it. Before Morgan reached the prelate, Father Christopher spoke.

"Hello, Mike. You've come to tell me something. What is it?"

Morgan shook his head.

"You're really something, Father, and I'm going to miss you."

"Miss me? Lovely thought. I miss you, too. Now, I've got something to tell you."

"No, Father. I said I will miss you because I'm leaving the seminary."

"Is it the girl?"

"Yes. I love her."

"I know."

"And I must leave."

"Hard to tell. You know the old saying: it's very difficult to prophesy, especially in regard to the future."

"I'm serious, Father. And this is important."

"Yes. Well, we better not waste any time. This might be the last lesson I can teach you."

Father Christopher admired the hammer in his hands. "This is a straight clawed hammer, a little dull. Claws were a necessary invention after someone figured out how to make round nails with heads on them. You can put the head of the nail between the claws and pull the nail out of a piece of wood."

He demonstrated on an invisible nail, pulling on the wooden handle, rolling the head against the bench. He got off the stool and walked to the grinder.

"But the hammer lost something – the ax. Claws are good for pulling nails, but not so great for shaping wood. Rigging ax was better. Of course, mills planed the lumber square and carpenters didn't need to trim planks too much. Then power saws, and drills, and . . . ."

"Father," Morgan interrupted, "what are you talking about?"

"Oh, yes. This is a good hammer head. Balanced. Solid. And look at these claws, long and a good line. The point is, you've got to keep them sharp. You never know when you'll need to cut something."

Father Christopher switched on the grinder. He kept it oiled and clean, and it hummed with magnetic efficiency. He held the back of the claws against the grinding wheel and sparks flew down in a winged pattern, bright orange against the gray of the motor housing. He pulled the hammer away and lifted the head to his eyes.

"This might take awhile," he said. "Pull up a chair."

Morgan dragged the stool to the end of the bench.

"Got this wire disc on the other side. See, it polishes the metal."

Father Christopher touched the head against the spinning wire, and the metal began to shine.

"All right," Father Christopher said as he pushed the side of one claw against the grinding wheel. "Here's your lesson. Once upon a time there was a young monk who lived among his villagers in the foothills of the Alps. He was a holy monk, knowing dreams and miracles."

Father Christopher pulled the hammer from the grinding stone and held it to the wire disc. It began to look new, sharp-angled and true.

"Got to be careful you don't mar the wood," he said, pointing to the handle.

"Father, the story."

"Okay. One night, an angel appeared to him in a dream. The angel told him that a plague would come to his village. He told the monk that the autumn rains would carry a curse, and anyone who drank the water would go crazy. 'What should I do?' the monk asked the angel."

Father Christopher turned his full attention to the grinder. He touched first the tip of one claw, then the other, topside, backside, turning the metal slightly to create a fine angle at the point. He inspected his effort and walked around Morgan to retrieve a thin, triangular file.

"Can't get in the corners with the disc. Have to use the file."

With firm, forward strokes, he pushed the file to the inside where the claws separated.

"Father?"

"Yes, yes. The angel told the monk to make a cistern and fill it with good water and to cover it so that the cursed rain would not pollute it. The young monk obeyed. He chipped a large hole into the side of a hill, down into the stone. He made a large cover from oak strips he purchased from the casket-maker, and he hired the smithy to cover it with tin and solder to make it watertight. Throughout the summer, he made many trips from the community well, carrying two buckets of water each trip, along the narrow path, up the hill and back again. All day, every day, he toiled to fill the cistern. Of course, the villagers began to make fun of him. Naturally, when he tried to tell them that an angel told him to prepare, they said he was crazy."

"Naturally."

Father Christopher returned to the grinder and polished the hammer head a little more. He focused on the looks of it now, highlighting the delicate mold lines along the neck, touching the tips, one side then the other, never letting them burn, but encouraging them to the sharpness of a blade.

"When the autumn rains arrived, just as the angel predicted, they carried the curse. The monk drank only water from the cistern, but the villagers drank from the community well and sometimes from one of the streams nearby, and since rain mixed with all the water, the results were inevitable. The monk watched as first the blacksmith went mad, because his efforts made him hot and he drank more water than most. Then the tailor, the cobbler, the butcher, and eventually every villager. The monk watched until he was the only sane person, and everyone in the village behaved crazy except him."

Father Christopher turned off the grinder. He lifted the hammer in one hand, turned it, and watched the light glint off the smooth facets of gleaming metal.

"Ah!" he said.

"Is that it?" Morgan asked.

"Yes," Father Christopher answered him. "And it couldn't be better."

With that he swung the hammer near Morgan's elbow and the claws sank into the top of the workbench with a swift thud while the handle held in the air at a slight angle away from Morgan, erect and final.

"Geez, Father," Morgan said, twisting away from the bench. "I meant is that the end of the story."

"Sure, that's all. What more could there be?"

"What does it mean?"

"What do you think it means?"

"It could mean the monk is the crazy one."

"Yep. It could. You think about it, son. Meanwhile, it's time to talk to God."

Father Christopher grabbed the hammer head and pushed it from side to side to loosen its bite until he pulled it free from the table.

"I've been a little disappointed with the timing of things," Father Christopher said.

He stood next to Morgan, testing the balance of the hammer, loosening and tightening his grip.

Morgan looked at him, but he sat quietly, wondering what the story meant and if it meant anything at all.

Father Christopher placed the hammer on the bench and rolled up the sleeves of his shirt. He gazed at the completed crucifix at the center of the workbench. It looked crude, lovingly made perhaps, but artless. It looked more like a pagan idol than a Christian symbol.

"I've decided He was nailed through the wrists."

"What do you mean?"

"Christ. I've decided they nailed him through the wrists, not through the hands. That's why He hasn't given me the stigmata. I've been waiting to bleed from the hands. The real thing is bleeding from the wrists."

"How did you come to that conclusion, Father?"

Father Christopher squeezed the hammer handle with his pudgy right hand and made a fist with his left hand.

"Sometimes you've got to prove your faith by action," he said.

He put his forearm on the workbench, leaning with his shoulder to force it down, his hand made into a fist facing up. Then, he swung the hammer, and the shiny, deadly claws sank into his stubby wrist slicing the skin and the artery. It settled with a thud through the flesh and into the ulna.

"Father!"

Morgan jumped from the stool.

The priest staggered backwards, awkwardly unbalanced and uncontrolled.

Morgan put his hands against the priest's back to steady him. With great effort, he then slid his hands into the priest's armpits and leaned his body against him to help him to the floor.

"Father, what have you done?"

"Act of faith," he said, but he groaned.

The shock attacked his heart, and he clutched his chest, his left arm motionless except for the trickling of blood.

"God, help me," Morgan said.

He grabbed Father Christopher's arm with one hand, and with the other, he yanked the heavy head of the hammer from the wrist. Instantly, blood spurted from the radial pulse.

"Lord Jesus," Morgan prayed, "don't let him die."

Morgan clutched the wrist with both of his hands, pressing against the wound to stop the blood flow.

"Heal him. Heal him," he said through clenched teeth.

The shock chiseled Father Christopher's face with dense surprise.

Morgan squeezed the wrist with more force, tensing his fingers and thumb into a tourniquet.

Father Christopher fought to breathe. His jaws locked and his tongue filled the cave of his mouth.

"Mmmm..."

Not an articulate sound. Mmmm, like a call, like a tribal aria, sacred and frightening.

Morgan pulled his hand away from the wrist to lift Father Christopher's head, and blood continued to crawl in a thick, cardinal harvest onto the harsh surface of the cement floor.

Father Christopher did not inhale, but his chest swelled. Then, with no announcement, no preparation, no warning, a protracted exhale forced the air from his lungs, emptying him.

The exhaustive exhale ended with a mild flutter of Father Christopher's lips, but Morgan could not, would not, recognize death.

"Do something," Morgan shouted.

Whether he shouted to God or at himself he didn't know, but for certain he felt fear, and panic drove him. He bent over the priest and pinched his nose. He took a breath and pressed his lips to Father Christopher's. He forced his exhale into the priest's mouth, and he watched the chest rise.

He lifted his head, and the chest fell as the air abandoned the lungs. He inhaled again and repeated the process, watching the chest rise; and, believing that the gesture forced life back into the dead body, he accepted the expunged air as if it were the priest's own.

Again and again Morgan breathed into the mouth, forcing his exhales past the swollen tongue, past the acrid smell of corruption.

As he prepared to offer breath again, a final expulsion of air and some undigested pork rushed from the priest's gullet, filled with bile, and Morgan could not prevent it, was, in fact, surprised by it, and the regurgitation blew into his own mouth, vile and corrupt. He pulled away, spitting, jumping away from the body, wiping his mouth, tasting the sour black decay deep against the porous surface of his gums, and even into the acid-filled recesses of his stomach. He spit again, fell to the floor and vomited air, his body struggling to expel the putrid taste. His knees scraped on the floor and tiny dimples in the concrete cut his skin, and the coagulating blood on his hands went cold.

The terror in Morgan's mind flushed any feeling of sanctity from him.

"God," he said. "Why don't You do something?"

The seeds of despair grow in such fertile moments, yet as he languished in the chasm of unreasonable loss, he noticed that Father Christopher seemed to be looking up at him, smiling.

At that moment, Morgan realized he must raise the priest from the dead. That is what healers do. He held his panic in check and closed his eyes to pray. He started with the Our Father, recognizing his appearance before the Divine, asserting the Divine as the Creator, trusting that the sound of God's name stirs miracle and power into the earthly realm. Thus, he began the process of invoking miracle. He prayed that God's will be done, through him, through his prayerful utterance, knowing that the action of God's will is miracle, knowing that the granting of miracle brings delight to the Father.

He knew that Jesus raised Lazarus from the dead, and he knew that the strength of Peter's faith freed the Father to use that faith to raise others from death.

"Use me now, Lord," Morgan prayed.

He looked at the body of Father Christopher, his muscles not yet suggesting rigor mortis. What would it feel like to see life return, to reclaim the lungs, the heart, the soul?

Suddenly, he felt paralyzing fear. He realized that an act of resurrection required a faith so substantial that it would separate him from others, for who would trust any such man?

If he could raise the dead back to life, others would fear him, not love him.

Others would come to him, but no one would ever give to him. He would spend the rest of his life giving unto others until nothing remained of himself, and he would disappear.

What kind of gift is that?

With swift, deadening wisdom, the complexity of faith became clear to him, and the enormity of it, and the frailty.

The fear of alienation proved more powerful than the excitement of miracle, and Morgan lost hold of the vision of God. Earthly concerns overwhelmed the morass of sanctification, and his faith diminished, weakened, and finally left him, oozed from him as the soul squeezed from Father Christopher. And without faith, what is left, for God rarely reveals His strength at times of cowardice.

"I'm sorry, Father," he said. "It's too much to ask."

He held the priest and brought death to his embrace.

CHAPTER 19

ALL CIRCUMSTANCES OF MORGAN'S LIFE remained intact, same parents, same brothers, same schoolmates, same teachers, same buildings, same sun and sky. All but one. Father Christopher was gone. And that one loss diminished all that remained; diminished Morgan in some unexplainable way as if a necessary part of him were removed, a thumb or a foot. But he felt the loss in his spirit also, as an inconsolable void. One great change changes all.

Answerless questions troubled his peace. He prayed; yet he agonized. He did not know what to do.

That Saturday afternoon, during work detail – with Father Christopher gone, what could he do? – he walked to the orchard and looked out across the autumn landscape. He watched a noisy formation of Canadian geese fly overhead, their calls argumentative and sharp. He grabbed a red apple from the ground and bit into it, but sour juice troubled him, and he spit it out. Two mourning doves flew along the stream, darting toward and then away from one another. A fish jumped, and the ripples spread out and away from the splash. The air smelled of death with the ashy odor of fallen leaves.

Nadine saw him from her steps and waved. He watched her. She did not run, but walked, and although her step looked lively, something different augmented her stride, a caution perhaps, like a sliver in her toe. He knew they had to make plans, make decisions, but he fought the urge to go to her.

As she came near, Morgan noticed that her cheeks looked puffy.

"Have you been crying?" he asked.

"No."

"What's wrong?"

"Nothing. We heard about Father Christopher."

"I cried for him all night," Morgan said.

"You must miss him."

"I want to spend this weekend with you. The funeral is Monday. Let's run away, go somewhere, just the two of us."

"Morgan," she said, "that sounds like fun, but we can't."

She sat down. Morgan slid his back against the tree and sat too, fumbling with his emotions. She did not look directly at him, but she sensed his need, and she rested her hand on his thigh. He turned his face into her shoulder and cried.

Soon, he lifted his head.

"I'm sorry," he said.

Nadine, too, had tears.

"Nadine, will you marry me?"

"Oh, Morgan," she said, "not right now. Maybe some other day."

"I'm serious."

"Of course you are. But today's a bad day to talk about marriage." Before he could reply, she continued. "I have an idea."

"What?"

"Let's go swimming in the quarry pond."

"What? No."

"Why not? You afraid?"

"Nadine, there are too many people around."

She sat up. "Come on, Morgan. That could be as adventurous as a motel room. Besides, it's Indian Summer, the last swimming days of the year."

Morgan wanted to hold her, and he wanted her to hold him. He needed comfort, not excitement. Why could she not see that?

"I don't feel like it," he said.

"I know," she teased, "it's the ghost. You're afraid of the ghost."

"Don't make fun, Nadine. He just died."

"Who?"

"Father Christopher."

"You afraid of him, too? I meant the child of slate."

"I'm not afraid," he insisted.

"Let's go then."

"I can't. I could get in trouble with Father Gale."

"I'm not afraid of him or the ghost. Besides, if you are leaving, what trouble can you get into?"

"Nadine."

She insisted on playing.

"My friend, Julie, knows this guy. He graduated a few years ago. Well, him and some of his friends went to your pond one night. And this is a true story. While they were swimming, they heard this weird whispering noise. Julie says they were drinking and it was probably just the wind. Anyway, they left and went to their car. They drove the back road down by the park, and they saw a hitchhiker, so they picked him up. They said he had real white skin and he didn't talk and he was spooky. All of a sudden, it was like something made everybody have to pee at the same time. So they stopped the car and they all got out and went to the side of the road. But when they were done, the hitchhiker was gone. They looked around for him, but he had disappeared.

"And guess what?"

"What?"

"They realized they had stopped the car right across from the old farm house that Francis Eastbrook lived in. They all jumped into the car and got away from there as fast as they could. And they never went back to the pond, either."

Morgan looked around as if he had a secret.

"I saw where he's buried," he said.

"Really?"

"Yes."

"Oh, Morgan. Take me there. I want to see it."

"No way. I don't want to go there. I'm afraid something will happen."

"Nothing will happen. What can happen?"

"I don't think so."

"Why'd you tell me, then? You haven't been there, have you?"

"Yes I have."

"Well?"

Morgan wrestled with conflicting thoughts. On one hand he did not like the idea of tempting Francis Eastbrook's ghost, or Father Christopher's. On the other hand, he wanted to please Nadine, to know that he could comfort someone. Maybe that would help comfort him.

"Okay," he said. "But you've got to be quiet and fast. I don't need any more trouble right now."

"I promise," she said, jumping up and hurrying toward the tennis court. Morgan slithered from tree to tree, hiding behind each one, hoping his invisibility would hide Nadine as well. They walked close to the walls of the building. Morgan kept putting his finger to his lips to hush her, but her eyes sparkled with excitement.

Morgan unlatched the shop door with both hands to quiet the hinges. He pulled the door open and went in. He flicked the light switch and found the lantern. After he lit the wick, he slid the glass cover into place and walked to the tunnel door.

"This way."

He unbolted the lock. As the door creaked open, Morgan's stomach filled with acid, and his throat constricted.

"I don't know, Nadine, maybe we shouldn't."

Nadine held his arm and pulled him forward.

"Come on," she said.

They walked along in the dampness. The lantern jiggled, and

reflections scampered across the walls. He steadied the handle.

Francis Eastbrook, he thought, if you are here, don't tell me.

Before they reached the opening at the end of the cave, they heard the cry of wind, moaning like the limbs of an aching spruce.

"What's that?" Nadine asked.

"Only the wind," Morgan said.

The light at the entrance began to displace the gloom of the lantern fire, and just before they reached the small ledge along the cave wall, Morgan stopped.

"Over there," he pointed. Nadine looked. "See the area of crushed gravel? That's where he's buried."

Nadine held his arm with both of her hands while she looked.

"Are you sure?"

"Father Christopher said so."

She nodded.

Sunlight brightened the entrance and sparkled across the top of the water in the pond beyond.

"I feel a chill," Nadine said. "Do you think it's him?"

"No," Morgan replied. "It's fear."

She hit him on the shoulder with one hand, but she continued to hold him with the other.

"I don't believe in ghosts," she said. "But do you think the dead return to haunt people?"

"I don't know. I don't like to think about it."

"I hope not," she said.

They walked to the ledge and sat down, both of them staring at the unmarked grave.

"Do you believe his ghost is around here?" she asked him.

"I don't know. Some people do."

"Why?"

"The stories, I guess."

"Tell me one of the stories."

The sun heated the stone around the entrance, and they began to feel the warmth against their legs.

"They say old Brother Giles knew the guy it happened to. It was right after they built the addition to the main building, back in the thirties. This one seminarian had decided to leave, and he was telling everybody. Said it was a lousy place and the ghost was stupid and stuff like that. He was riding the elevator up to his dorm. Students aren't supposed to use the elevator, but he was leaving, and he didn't care."

Nadine crossed her legs and sat straighter.

"Between floors the elevator stopped. The guy pushed all the buttons, but it didn't move. He pushed the alarm bell over and over, but it made no sound. He got frightened after a while, and he said, 'Okay, what do you want?' He looked around. The light stayed on, but the elevator did not move. It remained eerie and quiet. 'All right,' he screamed. 'This is a great place. I won't say anything bad about you. I promise.' Then quick, just like that, the elevator lurched and took him up to the second floor."

"So?" Nadine said.

"That's not all," Morgan continued. "Every once in a while, the elevator will go up or down by itself, and the doors will open, and no one will be inside. Especially at night."

"That doesn't sound so scary."

"It can be, especially late at night, with the great silence in the halls, and no one around. You can be walking to the bathroom and pow! that elevator door screams open!" He grabbed Nadine's arm, and she jumped off the ledge.

"Damn, Morgan." She hit his shoulder again.

"There's more," he continued. "They say he can make you do things you don't want to do."

"Oh? Like what?"

"Like swimming in his pond when you're not supposed to."

She laughed, and the laughter helped them relax.

Morgan tried to imagine a life with Nadine and what it would be like away from the seminary. He imagined endless days accentuated with moments like this one, both of them happy, without a care.

Nadine interrupted his reverie.

"Come on," she called.

He turned in time to watch her jump into the water, churning the surface to waves. She wore only her bra and panties, and when she came to the surface, half way across the pond, she raised her arm and called again.

"Come on in."

Morgan removed his clothes, down to his undershorts, and followed her. The water felt warm, heated in its gray, stone bowl. He sucked in a deep breath and let the water cascade from his head, down his face, into his eyes and his mouth. He felt revived, baptized again among the living.

Nadine swam to him, put her arms around his neck. He held her waist as they sank into gray-green mirth, and through the opaque sparkle, they smiled. They let go of each other and rose, sucking in breaths; then they slid down again into the suspended silence below the surface. For half an hour they played, throwing handsful of water high into the air, watching the droplets splatter against the surface. They laughed and listened to their echoes slide along the cliff edge. For a small moment in the eternal passage of time, they shared solitude, and they were able, in their play, briefly to lay aside their burdens.

When they came out, they sat on a slate outcropping and let their feet dangle into the water. They looked at each other and became aware of their youthful elegance, chilled by the brisk air and only marginally hidden by thin, wet undergarments.

He looked at her, beautiful and wet. The tipends of her hair released silver droplets along her back and shoulders. He moved his hand to hers. The sun warmed their skin, and for a moment the complexity of life gave way to a moment of simple tenderness, one person to another, lacking all need for explanation or understanding.

"I love you," he said.

"I know." But she did not look at him.

"What's wrong?" he asked.

"Morgan." She hesitated. She shook her head and looked at him. "It's nothing. Just hold me."

He held her, listening to her breath, accented by the wind, full of life. The strength of youth lies in its last great push to maturity, a strength of vitality uncomplicated by thought. The forces of life demanded their attention, and they luxuriated in their passage, without understanding, and yet, without fear, for life favors continuation, and their passion had released them from childhood. For long moments they remained, eyes closed to the future and perhaps even to the past.

Suddenly, she lifted her head. The sky suggested twilight.

"I've got to go," she said.

They dressed and walked quietly through the tunnel, not knowing that such moments of comfort come rarely.

When they reached the workshop door, they were not alone.

"Mr. O'Bryan," Father Gale said. "What is the meaning of this?"

Morgan turned quickly, frightened, embarrassed. He let go of Nadine.

"What are you doing in here?" Morgan snapped.

"That's none of your concern, young man," Father Gale said. "Although you might recognize that Father Christopher did have other friends besides you."

Nadine looked back and forth between them.

"I expect an explanation, Mr. O'Bryan," Father Gale said.

Then he spoke to Nadine.

"And you, young lady. . ."

Before he could finish, Nadine interrupted. "Oh, no you don't," she said. Her nose flared, and her eyes darted as if judging another runner in a race. "I don't want anything to do with this discussion or with you."

She moved away from Morgan.

Father Gale said, "Just one moment."

But Nadine ran to the door. She pushed it open and darted away before it closed behind her.

Father Gale and Morgan stood silently for a time.

"Morgan?"

"How could she leave me like that?" Morgan asked.

Morgan stared at the tools on the wall but did not focus on anything specific. He turned his head to look at Father Gale.

"She knew I could get kicked out of school. How could she just leave me like that? I want to leave, but I don't want to get expelled."

Morgan looked blankly at the floor and shook his head.

"Morgan," Father Gale said gently, "I don't think you're going to be expelled for your actions, but you may leave on your own."

Morgan looked at him.

"No one chooses a life of celibacy without much confusion and thought."

"You're not kicking me out?"

Father Gale shook his head.

"Why?"

"The desire for a woman is normal. God ordained it. Celibacy is abnormal. It requires a devotion to others powerful enough to accept Divine love in place of human comfort. So you don't get expelled for loving, but you must decide how you will express your love."

Oddly, Father Gale did not bring up psychology, although Morgan suspected he wanted to.

Before he left, Father Gale looked around the shop.

"I spent many hours in here, you know. I miss him, too."

The light bulb reflected in amber patterns along the stone, and Morgan looked into the shadows of the mortar joints. He knew the uneven plane of the wall, and he thought of the times he came to this place for consolation. But suddenly, he felt lonesome, and the fear of a life alone made a bitter taste rise in his mouth, like spent pork and bile. Nadine's abandonment of him hurt more than all the hurt he had compiled on the lonely bus rides from Galeton. And Father Christopher's death? An abandonment too. People remained undependable and God remained invisible. What could he make from such insubstantial clay? If the strength of a man is measured by his ability to carry loss, Morgan feared that trepidation and cowardice would ruin him.

CHAPTER 20

ON MONDAY MORNING, several hours before the Requiem Mass, Morgan sat on a bench at the side of the altar. Because of his friendship with Father Christopher, he would act as the main server. The funeral home brought the casket containing Father Christopher's body and lifted the casket onto the church truck. They pushed it into the chapel and up the aisle to the altar. Morgan noticed the wheels of the truck did not squeak, and he thought Father Christopher would like that. The undertakers genuflected and left. When the doors closed, Morgan felt the sanctity of the chapel, maybe because Father Christopher was there, maybe because he tried to visualize heaven and the actual procedure Father Christopher would follow as he entered. Are the gates real gold? Gold is heavy and soft. He wondered if such gates would sag. Too bad for Saint Peter if they did. Father

Christopher wouldn't tolerate shoddy workmanship.

The only light in the chapel came from the illumination behind the stained glass windows. A mosaic of filtered patterns played colorful silhouettes against the walls and along the charcoal shimmer of the terrazzo floor.

Morgan moved his hand to touch the folded funeral pall on the seat next to him. The soft sound echoed off the high ceiling like a frightened pigeon. Morgan, surprised by the sound, flinched.

"Well, Father Christopher, I better get started."

He lifted the funeral pall, an armful of elegant white linen with thick brocade trim. He pulled it over the casket and straightened the ends so the black embroidered cross lay centered. "Here's your travelling robe," he whispered.

But grief overcame him, and he sank his head into the cradle of his forearms.

He shut his eyes tight with a fierce will to close out the world and to hide in the emptiness of his loss. A darkness of solitude enveloped him, covered him in a living pall, and he submitted to it. His body shook with an odd serpentine distortion, and he felt his muscles contract.

Yet, without bidding, and mysteriously, his mind stopped

struggling. Whether from the climatic ceremony of closure about to begin, or from the exhaustion of loss, he recognized that the experience of calm in which he found himself was not of his own making. This knowledge did not alarm him, although it suggested a spiritual component. He felt no fear, and his anguish subsided within the silence.

In this momentary state of unexplainable elation, he asked the Spirit, "What does this mean?" The Spirit gave no verbal response. Instead, Morgan's body felt stretched, elongated, re-formed into an unrecognizable newness, and in that instant of unsubstantiated time, his mind recognized and accepted a feeling of God's unyielding constancy, a wisdom akin to knowing the sun would rise tomorrow in spite of any earthly suggestion to the contrary.

This sensation of acceptance, this spirit without form, dispersed before he could claim it, before he could wrap his arms around it and pull it into himself so that it would become a permanent aspect of his heart.

He lifted his head, and his eyes adjusted to the filtered and colored light of the chapel.

"What just happened?" he said out loud, and in his puzzlement, he focused on the wrinkles his grasping hands left in the funeral cloth.

It was a momentary dream, of course, but one of such visceral fortitude that he struggled to maintain his balance as he stepped away from the casket.

He smoothed the wrinkles and checked to see that no one had witnessed his display of emotion. Although he saw no one, he felt a low, droning sound in his head. He turned to the left, to the right, in a circle, but the chapel appeared empty.

"Damn, Father, for a second there I thought you were pulling one of your stunts."

"Not him. Me."

The voice startled Morgan, and he turned to see Peter Di Flavio. He walked from behind the mahogany prayer screen and came toward the altar.

"Thought you got rid of me, didn't you?"

Morgan stared across the casket.

"I thought you left."

"You thought I got kicked out, you mean. I can't let that go unpunished."

"What are you talking about?"

"Gale's not stupid, Morgan. He could see what was going on. Why didn't you stand up for me?"

His raised voice reverberated. Even the scraping of his shoes scratched in fearsome sound as he walked closer.

"Oh, he started out smoothly enough. Asked me if I thought my vocation was sincere. Asked if I'd been getting enough sleep. But he was prying into my business. And I knew it."

"What does that have to do with me, Pete?"

"You think I don't know about you?"

Curiosity mixed with an odd fear, and Morgan felt a sense of premonition like the call the wind makes against the underside of leaves before a storm.

Peter's eyes opened wide and wrinkles of a hideous rage furrowed his forehead.

"After ten minutes of Gale's psycho-talk, I told him I was busy and got up to leave. 'Mr. Di Flavio, we're not through,' he said, and I laughed at him. I told him, 'Look, Father, I'm fine. Check with my friends. Ask Morgan. Really, I'm fine.' But he wouldn't listen and made me sit down."

Peter shook his head at the memory of it.

"Kept going on about my calling. Finally, we argued, one thing led to another, and he sent me to pack."

Peter took another step closer to the casket.

"Why didn't you go to him, Morgan? Why didn't you help me?"

"I didn't know anything about it, Pete. Nobody knew anything. You didn't come to breakfast. Someone said he heard you had a fight. But that's all there was. A rumor."

Peter smiled, his white teeth sparkled. He put his hand up to indicate that Morgan should stop talking.

"It's all right, buddy," he said. "I don't want to hear any lies." He pointed an accusatory finger. "I will get even."

He turned away from the casket and walked out. The door closed with a muffled thud that Morgan felt in his ears and in his stomach.

Peter had stayed only a few minutes, but it felt as if much time had passed. Out of a concern for lateness or as an excuse to take his mind from Peter's apparition, Morgan returned to the preparations for Father Christopher's ceremony. At the same time, in the back of his mind, the strange dream of the Holy Spirit would not go completely to rest.

He lit the candles and brought the chalice and a canister of wine to the altar. He arranged five chairs so the priests, servers, and he could sit during the eulogy. He adjusted some of the flowers, turning one vase to the left, another to the right. He looked up at the crucifix. He wanted to run away, back to a time before Father Christopher's homemade stigmata. Instead, he walked to the sacristy to dress for Mass, a Requiem for his lesson-master, forever gone.

Morgan led the procession of servers and priests. He carried a small candle, a light leading the way. Behind him, the two minor servers walked with folded hands. Following them, the three priests who would con-celebrate the Mass: Father Superior, Father Gale, and Father Mark, an old friend of Father Christopher's from Boston. Father Gale carried the censer. The smoke from the incense curled through the air. They walked the few steps down the hallway, and Morgan waited for the procession to form a straight line. The great wooden doors of the chapel were braced open, like wings. Inside and straight ahead, Father Christopher's coffin sat on the church truck. The priests and brothers waited near chairs at the side of the altar, and the students filled their seats along the walls.

Father Gale coughed, indicating to Morgan that he should proceed, and as he walked past the doors he could see that the visitors' pews were full of townspeople who knew Father Christopher. Morgan was astonished to see his mother and his aunt on one side of the aisle, and even more astonished to see Nadine in the pew across the aisle. Peter Di Flavio stood next to her. Morgan's mother frowned at him, Nadine looked at him, and Peter stared at him with a smile that was not friendly. Morgan, trying to look straight ahead and to both sides simultaneously, inadvertently blew out the flame of his candle.

The students sang the "Miserere," and the youthful harmony of adolescent voices blended with the sonorous voices of the older prelates and filled the room with monastic tranquility. Morgan could not keep from looking at the visitor's pews. He could think of nothing more distracting at Father Christopher's funeral than the concurrent manifestations of his mother, his aunt, Nadine, and Peter Di Flavio. He began to compose possible dialogues with his mother and with Nadine. All of them concluded with Morgan running away. He became lost in speculation, and the entire first half of the Mass passed without his notice, so much so that at the consecration, Father Gale had to cough twice to get Morgan's attention so he would ring the bell.

Father Gale also raised his right eyebrow.

Before Father Superior broke the host, he stopped the ceremony to say a special remembrance for Father Christopher.

At the conclusion of the service, Morgan led the procession out, and as he neared the lay screen, Mrs. O'Bryan eased out of the pew, dragged her sister along by the hand, and walked along with her son.

"Morgan . . ."

"Mother, let's talk outside," he said, gesturing with his head back toward the procession.

Morgan nudged his mother in the direction of the main rotunda. One of the servers took the candle from Morgan so he could stay with his mother, and although the rest of the entourage went on to the sacristy, Father Gale remained in the rotunda and walked over to their group.

Father Gale moved them toward the front office so they wouldn't block egress from the chapel. After a moment, Nadine walked up to Morgan and smiled at him although she held back somewhat and allowed Peter to hold her arm in his, like a big brother walking his sister home from school.

At first, no one spoke.

Aunt Lillian broke the awkward silence.

"Morgan, I believe you've grown a foot since Christmas."

In fact, he had grown another four inches, and that made him over six feet tall, and he had gained nearly twenty pounds. His mother noticed too.

"You are bigger, son," she agreed.

He was taller than everyone in the group, and even wearing a cassock, he had the look of a maturing young man.

"Mother, Aunt Lillian, Father Gale, this is Nadine Shearwater. And I believe you all know Peter Di Flavio."

Turning to Nadine, he said, "I'm surprised to see you. Peter, what's going on?"

"Peter has been telling me so much about you, Morgan," Nadine answered. "We've become good friends. And I want to talk to you."

"What are you doing here?" Mrs. O'Bryan hissed.

Nadine took a step back.

"Now, Annie," Lillian said.

"Get away from my son, daughter of Eve."

"Mrs. O'Bryan, please." Father Gale turned to Morgan. "This is irregular, Morgan. We'll certainly need to talk about this. And Mr. Di Flavio . . ."

Morgan pulled Nadine aside. "I'm sorry," he said. "Can I meet you outside?"

"Okay," she said, and she and Peter walked away.

Morgan turned back to the group.

Father Gale, unaccustomed to being interrupted, suggested, "This could be an impulse neurosis."

"Don't start with me," Mrs. O'Bryan countered. "Morgan, what do you think you are doing?"

Morgan stared at her.

"Father, is there a place we can go to sit down?" Aunt Lillian suggested.

"Yes. In the office."

"Come along, Annie."

Father Gale directed Morgan to clear the altar and to put things away.

"We will talk later," he said.

Morgan nodded, but as Father Gale began to close the door, Morgan stopped him.

"Excuse me, Father," he said, and he walked in. "Mother, I want you to go home now. This is not a good time for you to be here."

For several startled seconds they all waited. Morgan looked authoritative in a way that arrested discussion.

"Morgan," his Aunt began.

"Not now, Aunt Lillian," he said, and he walked out the door.

CHAPTER 21

RESPONSIBILITIES OF THE MOMENT pressured his time. He cleaned the altar and made it ready for Mass the next morning.

When he finished, he sat in a chair, the silent chapel now an empty cave. He imagined, with a mixture of sadness and resignation, Father Gale would send his mother and Aunt Lillian away. He imagined watching the car, the small blue and yellow license plate growing smaller and smaller until it disappeared hopelessly out of sight.

It occurred to him that whenever his mother or his family came to the seminary to visit him, every time they left it was like a death. Yet, his bonds with them were familial, not intimate, forged over the years by memories separated by time. As a result, they no longer knew him, and, he realized, he did not really know them.

What sort of revelation is it when you look into your mind and realize you do not know your own family? This would never change, for the accumulation of his history no longer resembled that of his clan. He had grown individuated, and the needs of youth no longer bound him to home. He was severed, though he did not know it.

He had no control over these concerns, and although they plagued his thoughts, his desire to see Nadine overwhelmed them. What could she possibly be thinking appearing at this most sacred funeral ceremony? Did Peter put her up to something?

He walked out into the rotunda and out the front door. He stood on the entrance porch to look around. At the end of the long, curved driveway, Father Gale stood near Nadine's Triumph talking with Peter.

Nadine stood off to the side, leaning against a tree. She seemed preoccupied and appeared to ignore Father Gale and Peter.

Morgan headed down the drive. He walked past Father Gale, and he ignored Peter. He went directly toward Nadine, but Father Gale suddenly included him in his discussion.

"And, Mr. O'Bryan, no matter what the cause, this behavior is disruptive. It upsets the other students and intrudes on our monastic calm. Conclude your discussion as rapidly as possible and return to your room. I will meet with you later."

He then returned to Peter.

"As for you, Mr. Di Flavio, I will indulge your impertinence no longer. You will come with me, and I shall phone your father."

He waited for Peter to walk ahead of him.

"Good bye, Nadine," Peter called over his shoulder. "Good luck telling Morgan about the baby."

At that, Father Gale stiffened.

"Come along," he said.

Morgan looked from Nadine to Peter, at Father Gale's back as he herded Peter toward the school, and back to Nadine.

"He wasn't supposed to tell you."

"Tell me?"

"About the baby."

"Why not tell me? I think it's wonderful if we're having a baby."

He reached to hug her. She allowed the gesture but did not return it.

"I tried to tell you at the pond."

He nodded. "I knew something was bothering you."

She looked down.

"It's going to be okay," Morgan said.

"Morgan, stop."

"What is it?"

"I'm trying to tell you. There's not going to be a baby."

He looked puzzled.

"Peter has been a true friend. We met a few weeks after you returned from the novitiate. He told me you were friends. He's told me all about you, and I feel like I know you and your family better now because of him."

"Peter?"

"Yes. He truly cares about you. When I told him I was pregnant, he said it would really hurt if you found out. And since I couldn't talk to you about it, naturally, I talked to him."

"I don't think I'm getting this. Why wouldn't you talk to me?"

"Morgan, I can't marry you. I don't want to marry you. You're kind and good, but we're different. And we're too young. I can't marry you, and I can't have a baby."

"What do you mean?"

"I aborted the baby, Morgan. Peter helped me. He took me to see someone."

"That's not friendship, and you can't just dismiss my baby."

"I know you're upset. But you'll get over it. We both will. I love you, Morgan, but I've got to go. I'm sorry."

She turned her face away from him, as she opened the car door.

Stunned, he could not move. Nor could he speak, for he could not gather the fullness of the information he had just heard.

She looked up at him, her eyes tender, her voice soft, but like a vanishing whisper.

"I'm sorry."

She closed the door, and the metallic clasp resounded in his head, not like words, rather, like an echoing sound of death.

She drove away, sped down the roadway, and the throaty exhaust of the sports car blended into the western shadows and disappeared with the same severe suddenness that childhood ends.

Morgan's sense of balance faltered. He staggered and lunged against the tree. He leaned into it for support. He lost the balance in his reason as well. Anger overcame calm, and vengeance dispelled righteousness. Agony at Nadine's departure and the loss of a child diminished him, and a red fury commanded him.

He trampled up the drive, his eyes salted blind, and his teeth ground together so hard the muscles of his head tensed all the way to his neck.

Peter Di Flavio sat on the lower step, and as Morgan neared the staircase, Peter rose to meet him.

"Hey, buddy. No foul deed goes unpunished, eh?"

Morgan did not answer him. Instead he grabbed Peter so tightly that between the impact of Morgan clutching his shirt and the pressure of Morgan's arms in tension, Peter lost his breath.

"Why, Peter? Why?"

Morgan found no truth in Peter's eyes, only betrayal. The structure of his emotions turned to revulsion, and he pushed Peter away as if he were poison.

Peter, overwhelmed by Morgan's strength, tripped and stumbled. He cut his forehead against the corner of a stone step, but he did not move, for he dared not tempt the menace of Morgan's wrath.

Father Gale hurried with as much quickness as obesity allows.

"Morgan," he shouted, but Morgan had already quit the attack.

Morgan remained lost in turmoil, his spirit hollowed out, ready to shatter. Mere violence could not heal the agony he carried. He walked away.

Father Gale turned his attention to Peter.

"Mr. Di Flavio," he said, "you appear to have fallen. Are you ill?"

Peter made no attempt to move, and Father Gale made no attempt to help him.

"Your father will be here soon," Father Gale continued. "When you've cleaned yourself, we need to discuss the possibility of an intrapsychic need to injure yourself."

Father Gale attempted to usher Peter Di Flavio up the steps and into the building. Though momentarily cowed, Peter recognized that Morgan was no longer a threat, and he regained his rebellious attitude. He sat up, looked to make certain Morgan had quit his presence, and he began to berate the priest, shouting, threatening.

"That will be enough, Mr. Di Flavio," Father Gale said.

Morgan, mired in disillusion, ignored their dispute. He lumbered into an empty oblivion of extinguished love and unfair death, a forlorn plunge into hopelessness. The fear and betrayal which is loss oppressed him and tortured him with longing and desire for the unreachable.

He faltered without compass, utterly alone.

He shut his eyes, and a sudden, uninvited image of his infant child appeared; a myopic and blurry impression, lacking physical substance. A boy? A girl? A child. Our child. What do I know of you? What will I ever know of you? He could discern no clear picture, no vision, only a vague uncertainty that remained ever after an unfulfilled expectation and an everlasting ghost.

He staggered silently toward the only security he knew, Father Christopher's workshop.

As he walked, his anger turned on his faith. What kind of system

281

demanded that he love his enemy? A system that requires love to endure even unto treachery asks too much.

Morgan reached the shop door and went inside. Alone, in silence, he fell to the floor and heavy grief covered him as he huddled like an infant and cried deep into the night. He cried himself to exhaustion, and eventually to sleep.

CHAPTER 22

HE DID NOT KNOW how long he slept, but it was not eternal, for sometime deep in the night, he heard a rustling sound, and he awoke. His body remained fatigued, and the dangerous claws of despair clamped about his heart. He went to the wall and felt around for the light switch.

With the light on, he noticed the kerosene lantern on the workbench, a pack of matches next to it. He struck a match and lit the wick. When the fire flickered, he turned off the light.

The tangerine glow of ephemeral fire against the ancient stone of earth's core comforted him. Then he noticed that the lock on the door to the tunnel was open. Had he forgotten to secure it? He walked over and opened the door. A fast wind spun around the jamb and swirled into the shop. It carried the smell of blackberries. Morgan pushed the door wide open and extended the lamp into the tunnel. He saw nothing past the light of the lantern except shadowy dullness.

He shook his head.

"What am I doing?"

He closed the door and clicked the lock. He put the lantern on the bench and the yellow and orange flame drew shadows at the edge of its light. He sat on the stool and put his head in his hands.

Feeling lonely?

Morgan looked up. What are you doing?

I've come to talk to you.

Are you a saint?

We're all saints, Morgan. Read your Bible. You don't have to die to be a saint. You just have to believe.

Are you here to punish me?

Punish you? Why would I want to punish you?

Because I failed you. I didn't heal you.

Oh, but you did heal me.

No, you died.

My body died; but you healed me, anyway.

How, Father?

You let me know the truth.

The truth?

Sure. You let me know God's real gift to me. I demanded a gift He didn't want to give, and I missed the gift He gave me.

What are you talking about?

The stigmata, Morgan. That wasn't the gift God wanted me to have.

It wasn't?

It wasn't. God's best gifts are the people He gives us.

I don't know if I'm interested in God or His gifts right now.

Not happy, huh?

Are you happy?

Me? I'm in heaven. Of course I'm happy. It's a nice place, heaven. Clean. Lots of food; cookies and chocolate milk. And God, He's got a sense of humor. Loves to laugh. Know what else?

What?

He likes music. Gave me a violin when I got here.

That's nice.

Did you know that the majority of the sound modes in a violin are transferred to the walls and then to the surrounding air?

I didn't know that.

Except for the Helmholtz mode. Helmholtz mode radiates out through the F holes.

Father.

What?

I don't know what to do.

Listen.

Listen?

Sure. God loves when His children listen. Listen like you listen to music; not with your head, with your heart. That's where God talks most clearly. You know, where love is.

My heart is no good, and love? I don't know about love. Besides, you talk like it's human love and not Divine love.

There's no difference. Did you know it can take two years just to get the finish on a violin?

What do you mean there's no difference? Isn't there a difference between the way I love God and the way I love Nadine? Or the way I used to love them. Or the way I tried to love them.

I don't know. You decide. First, you have to scrape the wood gently to raise the grain. Then you have to oxidize the wood, which turns it brown. Ozone gives each one a unique shade.

You mean it's okay if I love Nadine? How could He allow that after what's happened?

It's not a matter of permission, Morgan. Love is love. All it takes is courage. You don't need anybody's permission to love. It's a choice. You either love or you don't. What you do with it when you get it, well, that's when life gets interesting. Like the violin. You hang it in the sun and the UV rays form ozone when they strike the surface, oxidizing the wood. You never know what color you're going to get. You leave the raw instrument in the sun about one summer if you're near the equator; here in Pennsylvania, about a year.

Father, you're confusing me.

Don't worry, He understands.

If He understands, what am I going to do?

After a year in the sun, the wood will absorb moisture, especially in a place with high humidity, so it goes in the drying box for a month. Then it's ready to stain and varnish.

Father.

Don't interrupt. Here's the interesting part. The first two coats of varnish are applied, one after the other, to seal the wood. Again you hang it in the sun for a week to dry. Then you apply two more coats each with a week's drying time.

Father?

Loving effort takes time to reveal its beauty, Morgan. When those coats dry, the instrument is ready for the first coat of color. You squeeze about two inches of oil color from the tube onto a piece of window glass and mix in a little terpene-resin varnish. Working time is only two hours. Here's what's important. You use your fingers to apply the color, using a circular motion, moving constantly. You smooth out uneven areas with the heal of your thumb. Every little part, ribs and plates, F hole, peg box, and neck. All of it. You let it dry. Do it again. Let it dry. Four, five, six times. It takes another year.

Father, what am I going to do?

You'll know. Don't worry. That's what faith is, not worrying even when you can't see what's coming. Eventually, something will happen. It always does.

That's it?

After that, you want more?

Father, please.

Okay. How about this? What you love stains you.

I'll remember it always.

You're depressed, so I'll leave you with a gift. You've got to keep it; make it last. I don't know when I'll get back this way.

I can't go on.

You can. And you will. Now here's your gift. Close your eyes and don't be afraid.

Morgan closed his eyes.

The image of two starving children entered his mind. A young boy, perhaps seven years old carried a younger boy, maybe four years old. The older child had beautiful teeth. Yet the teeth were too large for his mouth, and he had an old man's face, etched with wrinkles of suffering. His body was thin, without muscle, tendon on bone covered with skin, a fleshly skeleton of haunting hunger. The child he carried rested his head on the shoulder of the older boy, his face not visible. Perhaps they were brothers. The backbone of the smaller boy looked like marbles pushing against his skin, and the skin strained around his arms and legs so tightly that Morgan could almost feel his elbow and his shoulder blades.

Their horrible thinness made them deathlike and tormented, yet he began to feel an acute empathy for the children. He began to ache for them, a physical soreness, like a compulsion of concern. He wanted them to know tenderness, wished they might know compassion. He wanted to give them water.

The vision then changed, and he was above them, looking down upon them from the cross. He did not feel pain, although he absorbed flesh-knowledge of every laceration and every thorn and nail of the hanging Christ. At the same time, he shared in the relentless and unlimited love that Christ felt for the two boys. Without judgment He loved them, their hungry skin, their thin-boned frames. He loved them more than they could love themselves, more than they could comprehend.

The mind of God filled Morgan, boundless, unchanging, a universe of love within his small heart. He became the universe itself, able to know the sorrow of another. He felt, within his own body, that each brutality of flesh contained within it the substance of forgiveness. This forgiveness infused him with peace, floating within a radiant burst of whiteness as if surrounded by a circle of brilliant suns. He was part of it now, part of every particle, every galaxy, and in that moment of connectedness, all anger, guilt, revenge, failure, even death, left him. This sensation penetrated every aspect of his nerves and every energy point of his spirit. In that moment, held within the compass of the universe, he understood that loving others, no matter the risk, that is the measure by which the Lord would judge his life.

The reality between the edge of thought and the crevice of imagination bent. The beatific sensation overwhelmed his logic to yield an inscrutable recognition and awareness, like knowing the movement of mountains. Morgan, the crucified Christ, the unknown others, momentarily transfixed and bound together like particles of cloud. Within that incomprehensible action of self-abandonment, loving his neighbor and loving God occurred in a simultaneous fracture, and Morgan's individualized self recognized its unique splendor, its eyes and arms and mind and soul.

He did not know the passage of time.

When he opened his eyes, his body did not ache. He looked around the red and yellow blush of flickering light, and encased within the workshop walls, he felt secure and apprenticed, but with his teacher now gone, he knew all the world had changed. It was the same for Moses upon his return from the mountain.

The gifts of wind and laughter were memorialized in his whispers and in his lungs, and he understood that the healing strength of memory must sustain him. The blessing of mystery begets indistinct recovery, and the knowledge of God felt particularly burdensome since he must carry as invisible proof that which remains invisible.

Morgan found composure enough to regain a sense of daily life, and life demanded attention. He walked out into the sunglow of the day. He did not shield his eyes from the command of its brightness, yet he stopped, momentarily stunned by its power.

"We have worried and prayed for you, Morgan."

"Father Gale?"

Morgan lifted his hand to shade his vision.

"You've been in there three days."

"Three days?"

"The door would not open."

"But the door lock is on the outside."

"Yes," Father Gale agreed. "A mystery of some ancient science, I suspect."

"I saw Father Christopher."

"Ah, yes," Father Gale said. "I too have seen visions. What can you reveal?"

"Once Father Christopher told me a story about a monk who was visited by an angel. The angel told the monk that a rain would come, and it would transform the water so that anyone who drank would go insane."

"Ah, yes, Paxon's famous Ambiguity Paradox."

"I never knew what it meant."

"No one does. It's an ambiguous paradox."

"I know what it means for me."

"Oh?"

"I must drink the rainwater."

"What do you mean?"

"I must leave here."

"No, Morgan, you must stay. The ways of the world are treacherous, and the ways of God mysterious. Here you will be safe."

Morgan smiled at the priest.

"I fear the shallowness of such safety, Father, when it would hide rather than protect. I walk a road unknown."

"The sun is setting."

Morgan stared at the pebbles of the walkway, the unity of which made a path, the individuality of each sharp edge, the enjoinment of many individuals in common bond. He pushed one foot against one pebble, scraping it into a new crevice, an act both destructive and creative in its action and in its consequence.

"I have a long road ahead, don't I?"

"Each road is long, Morgan. And singular. Let us begin with a short walk to the refectory. You must be hungry."

"I am hungry," he said.

"How about some sugar cookies and chocolate milk?"

"Sounds like a good start."

"Food avoidance can suggest some concern," Father Gale said as they walked to the kitchen.

"Oh?"

"Indeed. For instance, one might develop an obsessive compulsive aversion to food."

"I don't see that happening," Morgan assured him.

They reached the back entrance, and Morgan held the door.

They entered the kitchen, and Morgan gathered glasses and dishes.

Father Gale went to the walk-in for milk.

Morgan brought the canister of cookies to the table. He removed several and placed them on a plate.

Father Gale brought a quart of chocolate milk. He held the glass bottle with his right hand and began to undo the paper cap with his left hand. He flinched when he pulled at the cap.

"What's the problem?" Morgan asked.

"An eating disorder can cause anxiety, even depression."

"Father, what's wrong with your hand?"

"My hand? Nothing."

Morgan moved next to the prelate.

"Let me pour," he said.

Father Gale surrendered the bottle, and he sat down. In his effort to get comfortable in the chair, his sleeves pulled up, and Morgan saw a deep purple and gray bruise on Father Gale's right forearm.

Morgan poured the milk. He moved around the table and sat opposite the priest.

He pushed the plate of cookies across the center of the table toward Father Gale, offering one like a piece of bread at the last supper.

"I did this once with Father Christopher, you know."

"Yes," Father Gale said.

They grew quiet then, each with memories of a friend whose friendship they shared.

Father Gale sat back with his hands on his lap.

"It is not a stretch, Morgan," he said, "to suspect a passive suicidal ideation when it comes to food avoidance."

"What happened to your arm, Father?"

Father Gale pulled his sleeve to reveal the extent of his injury.

"The result of Mr. DeFlavio's rather uncivil response to my offer to escort him from the steps to await the arrival of his father."

"It looks like it might be broken."

"Likely. Will you have another cookie?"

Morgan declined. "It is time," he said. "Will you walk with me to the road, Father?"

"Yes."

They reached the front roadway, down which Morgan's chosen tomorrow led. He looked at the brick edifice which had become his home, the citadel of his education, and the foundation of his manhood.

"Your clothes? Belongings?" Father Gale asked.

"I'll send word."

Father Gale nodded.

Morgan stepped in front of the priest and held out his hand.

"May I?" Morgan asked.

Gingerly, Father Gale lifted his arm.

Morgan held the priest's hand, and he slid Father Gale's sleeve away from the injury.

"Lord, Jesus," he began.

Morgan wrapped his fingers around the wound, and gradually warmth penetrated the muscle. Painlessly, the bruise diminished, then disappeared.

Father Gale accepted this gift without comment.

"Go in peace, child of God," he said.

Morgan walked along the gravel roadway, in his periphery an orchard of apples, in his horizon dusk's rising stars. Of the cares he carried, loss of loved ones weighed the most, with the agony of empty promise its twin. Yet, into tomorrow he could now trudge, against the pitiless wind of solitude, carrying memory like a jewel, and fragile hope like a fledgling, and he knew he would find miracle there, if he dared the courage to believe.

THE END